CLANN

Ola Boutique

AN OLA BOUTIQUE MYSTERY

L. j. Charles

Caitlin's Tarot: The Ola Boutique mysteries are a spinoff series set in the Everly Gray Adventures world. These first three installments have been combined into a single book for the print edition. They need to be read in order.

1. The Fool
2. The Chariot
3. The Moon

To help my readers orient to Caitlin's world, I've included the *Everly's World Cast of Characters.* I hope you find it helpful.

Thank you for joining me in Caitlin's Escapades.

Happy reading,

L. j.

EVERLY GRAY'S WORLD
CAST OF CHARACTERS

Everly Gray: Red hair, midnight blue eyes, pale skin, of Scottish and Hawaiian heritage. Everly was born with ESP fingers. When she touches people or objects, she "sees" things about them.

Tynan Pierce: Black Irish with dark hair and azure blue eyes. Moves like the night and doesn't say much. Former agent with one of those three-letter agencies no one discusses. Pierce was Annie Jamison (A.J.) Stone's partner before she retired.

Everly's family:

Loyria and James Gray: Everly's parents (featured in *To Touch Poison*). Both were employed by the CIA, Loyria as a forensic anthropologist, and James as an attorney (his cover as a cryptologist). Loyria discovered a plant-derived formula similar to that used by Amazonian tribes in their euthanasia rituals. The United States government was interested in the formula and its potential for biological warfare, and joined with British and Irish intelligence to create the Megiddo Project, housed in a super-secret facility in the Amazon jungle. Loyria was the CIA member of the team, but she refused to release the formula until she had an antidote.

Kahuna Aukele: Everly's grandfather. A sixty-something Hawaiian shaman with a devious mind. He teaches kahunas-in-training by avoiding their questions, and forcing them to think.

Other characters:

Annie Jamison Stone Martin (A.J.): Blonde, light green eyes, retired sniper. Annie was Everly's next-door neighbor and is still her best friend. Soul sisters. Tynan Pierce's former partner in the world of dark and dangerous, Annie retired from the spy world, recently married firefighter Sean Martin, and they have a daughter, Madigan. They live in Hawaii's North Shore.

Adam Stone: Blond with brown streaks, dark green eyes. Annie's brother and a former homicide detective for Apex, NC law enforcement, currently working with the Honolulu Police Department. Adam follows procedure—always. He was Everly's mentor for police work, but recently moved to Hawaii to be near Annie and his new niece, Madigan.

Fion Connor: (*To Touch Poison*) A colleague of Loyria Gray on the Amazon-based Megiddo Project and an agent for MI6. Fion was the undisputed mistress and owner of a large estate near the English Riviera. Surviving her are her daughter Caitlin Eireen Connor, and a sister, Nolla Connor.

Eamon Grady: (*To Touch Poison*) Scottish, and the third member of the international team of scientists working on the Megiddo Project. Eamon was diagnosed with multiple sclerosis shortly after the project was underway. He would have done anything for a cure, and believed Loyria's formula was the answer.

The Fool

Caitlin's Tarot: Episode 1

You can never escape from murder...

At least that's how it seems to Caitlin Connor. Blessed with funky DNA, she's able to see auras, read Tarot cards, and oh, yeah, she also packs the powerful ability to manipulate energy—the same energy that was instrumental in her mother's death.

Ready for a new beginning, Caitlin leaves her estate on the English Riviera in her aunt's capable hands, and with a hefty dose of optimism, travels to Hawaii's North Shore to practice her newly learned art of reading Tarot cards.

Day one: Caitlin is faced with her personal prophecy. Day two: she trips over a dead body and hits the Honolulu PD's suspect list. Whoever said life in paradise was idyllic didn't know Caitlin Connor.

Can she find the killer and get on with living her dream, or will her future be limited to a jail cell?

Ireland, nine months previously...

IT WENT DOWN SOMETHING LIKE THIS:

I innocently served an American woman (Everly Gray) her first ever order of authentic fish and chips. It was my job, so no big deal, until we coincidentally became friends, and then she and her lustworthy significant other, Tynan Pierce, helped me escape my mother's evil clutches.

Not that I needed help. I'd been making the trip from England to Ireland to hide out in my father's house at the Tuatha Dé Danann commune since I was eight.

But then the Universe hit me with another coincidence. Everly and Tynan showed up at the very same commune. Yeah, it made me twitch, but they were nice people, not stalker types at all. At least I didn't think so, until she laid this killer—and I mean that in the literal sense—news on me.

"I'm sorry, Cait, but the evidence points to your parents working as a team to murder my parents."

My brain self-destructed for a solid five, maybe ten minutes. I knew my parents, Fion Connor and Eamon Grady, were evil personified, true enough, but until that moment I hadn't faced it square-on like that.

According to Everly, neither Eamon nor Fion was born crazy. That would've been too easy. Nope, my genetic donors had worked on some secret government project involving a weird formula, and apparently drank the stuff to gain paranormal powers. Ugly psychic power, not the nice sort like Gypsy women who told fortunes and wore a lot of bracelets.

After hearing this news about the depth of depravity festering in my sperm donor and my embryo incubator, I buried my shock beneath layers of denial, and innocently strolled into my father's house. I bypassed him and settled in my bedroom to think over how it might change my life, having murderers for parents.

Living with Fion had taught me the value of distraction when unpleasant thoughts took over my brain, so when I heard the guttural purr of a car engine, and tires crunching on gravel, I jumped off the bed, lifted the curtain, and peered outside. My mother's car was parked in front of the house. Shock, or maybe fear, clawed at me. To the best of my knowledge, it was the first time since my conception that the parents had been within shouting distance of each other. Their shared hatred was an undeniable fact.

Fion's boyfriend climbed out of the driver's side, helped her from the passenger side, and they headed toward the house. I strained to hear what they were saying, but couldn't, so I cracked the window open. It slid silently, but still my mother pulled the boyfriend to a stop, and stared at me. Her smile was dark and malicious, the stuff of nightmares. What the hell was she doing here?

I jumped back, dropping the curtain into place.

Escape. I had to leave. Now.

Footsteps pounded in the hall outside my bedroom door.

Panic shredded common sense, and I shoved the window open, stretching one leg over the sill.

My bedroom door crashed open, and the boyfriend's

beefy hand clamped on my shoulder. "Going somewhere Caitlin?"

I twisted, frantic to break his hold. A sharp sting bit into my neck. I slapped at it. Too late. My vision blurred, and I lost control of my muscles.

Bits of horrific memories will forever plague me about what followed. Fion and Eamon asked questions I didn't understand, and when I answered wrong or not at all, they gagged me and beat me. My wrists and ankles were scraped raw from the rough ropes they used to tie me down.

I remember the pain.

And the screams ripping my throat raw.

But my mind stayed numb, and my thoughts had been fuzzily incoherent until I opened my eyes to find Tynan Pierce standing next to the bed. *That* beautiful moment was etched in my memory.

I tried to smile, but couldn't make my lips work. He murmured things to me, and the sweetness of his Irish brogue seeped into me, calming me. He freed me, gave me a drink of water, then helped me to stand. "Hang on to me, Caitlin. You can't sleep yet. I'll get you out of here, and to my mother, but you need to help me."

I inhaled, calling on every ounce of strength I had to put one foot in front of the other. The blood on my hands made them slippery, but I clung to Tynan's belt. My lifeline. Walk. Stumble. But I didn't fall. And when I saw Everly, I attempted a smile. And tried to talk. "You're going to kill my parents, aren't you?" They weren't the words I'd intended to say, but they'd do.

She mumbled something.

I willed my tongue to keep working, to make her understand. "They were going to kill me. I knew my mother hated me, but my father, crazy bastard that he is, I didn't think... They need to be put down like rabid dogs."

Pierce caught me when I stumbled. "Doesn't mean you're like them, Caitlin."

There was something in his voice. I let go of the panic, and sucked in a full breath. Tynan didn't think I was ugly inside, and it gave me a surge of strength. "Siofra?" It came out a slurred whisper.

Tynan squeezed my hand. "She'll care for you."

Tynan's parents, Siofra and Lorcán Pierce, were my surrogate family, and they offered a safe haven from my father. Eamon was as crazy as Fion, so I normally avoided him during my visits by spending a lot of time in Siofra's kitchen. It was my hidey-hole, and had become the only real home I had ever known. Tynan's mother gave the best hugs, and she smelled warm and spicy. Safe.

Most of our walk to the Pierce household that night is still a blur, but I remember arriving and Siofra taking charge. I curled into a ball on the sofa surrounded by soft pillows, warm blankets, and her scent drifting around me. Her hands worked healing magic at my temples. I didn't want that dream to end, so I reached for sleep, and found it.

My recuperation was slow, and involved continuous bouts of nausea and vomiting. Siofra moved me upstairs to the guest bedroom when I became so terribly ill, and continually reassured me it was just my body getting rid of the drugs. Weak and battered, I slept on the bathroom floor, and lost track of everyone else in the household.

I slowly got better, moved into the bedroom, but could only stay awake for a few swallows of liquid before I fell into deep sleep. I missed a lot of what went on during my "druggie" time, even though Siofra tried to keep me up to date. Tynan had been hurt, but was healing well. Before I could stay awake long enough to make it down to check on him, I heard his voice blending with the others, so gave in again to my sore muscles and overwhelming exhaustion.

My escape into sleep ended abruptly when a commotion erupted. Fion's name stood out clear and strong in the conversations drifting up the stairs, so I planted my feet on the floor, and tottered for the shower.

By the time I got cleaned up and dressed, all was quiet. I bartered with myself and agreed to one more short lie-in before I re-entered community life and faced my mother. I desperately wanted to know why she hadn't been arrested yet, but granted myself a few minutes to prep. The shower and hair washing had worn me out, so I sprawled on top of my bed, and stared at the mesmerizing rhythm of the ceiling fan.

I deliberately got lost in the monotony of it. It was peaceful. And soothing. Two things that had been missing from almost every moment of my life to date, all two hundred and seventy-three months of it. I'd be celebrating my twenty-third birthday soon, and it was past time for things to change, for me to take a stand and permanently escape from the innate malice infecting both my parents.

Yep, Everly and Tynan had brought the bloody hash

of my dysfunctional family to a head. I swung my legs off the bed, stood, crept down the hallway, and sat on the top step. There were shadows concealing my presence, but I had a full view of the living room.

Everly, Tynan, and a blond woman Siofra had told me about, surrounded Fion. The blond woman had to be Annie, a spy-type who worked for Tynan. They worked like a well-rehearsed team, and had my mother duct-taped—wrists, ankles, and mouth. She squawked like a deranged hyena from behind the tape, and I nearly beat a hasty retreat back to the guest bedroom.

But that would have been cowardly, and I wanted, needed, Siofra, Everly, and Tynan to be proud of me. One foot at a time, I trudged downstairs. With each step it became more difficult to breathe, like the oxygen was being sucked from my lungs. It took me a minute to figure out why.

It was my mother's magic stealing my breath. Both Everly and Siofra were equally powerful psychics, and apparently that type of energy, whether dark or light, takes up a lot of air space. I barely managed two more pants before I realized Tynan, Annie, and Lorcán weren't gasping for air. At all.

Time to face up to the truth: I was hiding from myself. From *my* magic.

It wasn't exactly news. I'd been aware of my...unusual energy...from childhood, but I'd fought it with every bit of strength I possessed. I was determined not to be like Fion and Eamon. Not. Ever. And if it meant I had to shut out every aura that lit up a room, and stifle every wave of intuition gnawing at the pit of my stomach, so be it. I was a genetically altered witch, and with all that psychic energy floating around downstairs, try as I might, it was impossible for me to hide from it any longer.

Maybe I needed a Witches Anonymous meeting where I could make a simple announcement. I whispered it into the stillness and safety of the shadows. "Hello. My name is Caitlin, and I'm a witch." I gagged on the words.

And then the screaming started.

It was Siofra, and I ended up downstairs before I'd made a conscious decision to move. My inner witch must have recognized how much I loved my surrogate mother, and stepped into action.

A blast of my witchy energy mainlined adrenaline through my nerves.

Fion was using her synthetic Wiccan powers to levitate Siofra and crush her against a wall. The brutal force surrounding Siofra's limp body lifted the hair on my nape.

Everly's focus was centered on the malicious energy spewing from my mother. Intent brightened the midnight blue of Everly's eyes, and dazzling colors spun around her. She closed her eyes, drew in a long breath, and sent energy in a tight, sharp line directly at my mother. Fion immediately dropped Siofra, and began weaving a lethal pattern. It hit Everly square in the chest, but she'd managed to alter the energy grid, changing it from a weapon into a healing tool the barest second before it rammed into her.

The room crackled with blinding white energy.

So much energy. And for the first time, I was caught in the magic of it, unable to shut down, to close my awareness as I usually did. Instead, I opened my senses completely to watch and learn as Everly untangled Fion's destructive attack patterns almost as quickly as she created them.

But Everly needed help. And I had the genetic ability, and a hereditary understanding of my mother's dark energy. This was my destiny. It was probably one of those things the Universe set into place before my birth. I almost laughed. Like with Eve and the apple, Fion had chosen to drink the forbidden elixir, and used its power for harm. But it would end right here with me. There was no other option.

I reached for the dark energy pouring through my veins. Cold. I expected it to be ugly. Repulsive. But it was innocent, and only my actions, my choices, could make it loving or hateful. I held an image of the love I had for Siofra, strong and steady, until it fused with the dense strands of my mutated DNA. I didn't expect it to pulse with life, to seep into my bones, chill my body, and freeze time in slow motion, but it did.

I slipped my hand into Everly's. "This is my fight, too, El," I said.

It took me a minute to assess the combination of our innate energy patterns. Everly and I were *exact* opposites. Mirror images. My dense vs. her light. My grounded vs. her wispy. And together we were able to build a shield so strong and bright it mirrored Fion's lethal energy right back at her.

Everly tried to break free from my grip on her hand, but I held tight. My mother's death would rest in *our* hands. Not just Everly's. I'd have to tell her someday. My decision had nothing to do with death, but everything to do with life. If I didn't hold strong and control the darkness inside me, if I didn't infuse it with unbreakable love, it would suck me in and become an evil addiction just like the one that had controlled my parents for years. And I wouldn't allow that. Not now. Not ever.

When it was over, I looked down at my mother's body, watched the color drain from her aura, and her life force fade to nothing.

And then we had to deal with my father. It was a short confrontation, involving no magic whatsoever. There was a bit of a dust-up when he claimed to be Everly's father as well as mine, and I confess to a secret rush of excitement when I believed we might be sisters, but it was quickly sorted out that Eamon was truly Everly's paternal uncle. Just before Tynan cuffed him, my father managed to outwit us all, and threw a lethal dose of the elixir down his throat. It was...awful.

I learned two things from my parents' deaths.

First, there are no coincidences.

And second, my genetic predisposition to witchcraft needed to stay safely buried. I didn't make the decision lightly. If I used Everly for a role model, and it was tempting, I might be able to create some positive changes in the world. It was tempting, especially after working with her, because she'd showed me that my energy was more inside-out than dark and dense. It was more like the core of the universe. But I'd lived with the results when magic went wrong, so those new realizations didn't change my original plan to avoid magic.

I would embrace the basics of my inherited Craft, cast circles, clear my space of negative energy, and bless items. Scan auras too, but that fell into a slightly different category. I only had to skim the surface of my inside-out energy for enough power to do brief energy assessments of people. It bordered on iffy, but when I weighed it against personal safety, protecting myself won every time. Basically, my choice was to be nothing more than a stereotypical Gypsy witch...complete with silver bangles.

The Universe laughed.

Chapter 1

TWO OF WANDS

*Using one's intuition to search out
new possibilities and hidden options.*

MY ATTORNEY'S OLD-FASHIONED FOUNTAIN PEN WAS
fat and cumbersome in my hand, and the nib scratched
against the heavy paper as I scribbled my name...and
sealed my fate. Fingers trembling, I handed the pen to
Aunt Nolla. She nibbled at her bottom lip, concentrating
while she formed each stroke of her name, and finally
added a pretty flourish to the last letter.

I took it as a positive sign, and without the slightest
hint of regret slid the thick sheaf of papers across the table
toward my attorney. "Aunt Nolla and I are partners now,
Mr. Dobney, like we always should have been."

He cleared his throat, straightened the stack of papers,
and held his hand out for the pen. "Right, then. Goes
against your mother's wishes, but so be it."

Aunt Nolla's eyes faded to a dull brown, and I
struggled to keep from kicking Dobney's shins. If there
had been any way for me to switch attorneys, I would have.
Damn my female genetic donor and her will. I stood,
towering over the weasely Dobney. "It's my estate, and my

decision. I expect you to remain available to Aunt Nolla to help with any legal issues, and answer any questions she might have. Is that clear?"

He huffed, and flapped his outstretched hand at Nolla. "Yes, Miss Caitlin. I'll do my best."

Aunt Nolla stood, drew her shoulders back, and slapped the pen in his hand. When she glanced at me, the twinkle was back in her eyes. "I'm not bound by my sister's will, Mr. Dobney. If you're not able to support me and the estate, I'll find another attorney."

He backpedaled faster than I could down a pint of Guinness on a Friday night. "No, no. I'll be pleased to help. Ring me up whenever you need to." He shifted his chair back and stood. "Good day, ladies."

Aunt Nolla grabbed me in a hug. The first taste of freedom rocked my insides, and my feet tapped a bit of a jig, breaking our hug. "We did it, Aunt Nolla. Screwed Fion's intentions to bloody hell and back." I slung my duffle over my shoulder, and touched the corner of the Tarot deck poking against the fabric...my talisman. My new life. And all because of a broken shoelace, a crafty old man, and my inborn witch brewing her quiet magic.

I nodded toward the wall clock. "Almost time for my ride."

We headed outside, and Aunt Nolla pointed at my bag. "Did you already draw a card to start your journey?"

I lifted the deck from a zippered pocket of my duffle, and sorted through it. "Yes, and about went apoplectic. But it's not as bad as it looks." I turned the card so she could see.

She shook her head, making a tsk-tsk sound. "The Fool. Doesn't look like a good start, especially since that old man running the magic store isn't to be trusted. Who knows where he came from, hiding away in his creepy, run-down shop. Honestly, Caitlin, you should stay home with me. There's more room in the manor than either of us will ever need. Why, we wouldn't bump into each other for days unless we planned to."

Aunt Nolla hadn't set foot off English soil in all her forty-seven years, and never would. But I wasn't like her. "I can't stay here. Too many memories of Fion Conner, and besides, I have a new cousin to hang out with."

"You've been calling your mother by her full name since her death, and though a nastier person has never walked the earth, I do believe you need to talk to someone about it." She sniffed. "It's been nine months, Cait."

And I never would talk about it. What daughter wants to remember, much less discuss, being a key factor in her mother's death—well-deserved or not. I didn't have any regrets, and if the Universe offered me a do-over of the day Fion died, I wouldn't change a thing. Hatred and malice had found fertile ground and a cozy residence in both my parents, and the earth was a better place without them. Still, it wasn't something I wanted to discuss.

Aunt Nolla grabbed my hand. "Enough of the shuffling. Put those ghastly cards away before they make me any jumpier. You might well be playing the fool, Caitlin Eireen Connor, traipsing off to Hawaii to be near a woman who's a virtual stranger. Why, cousin or not, you don't even know for sure Everly Gray will keep her promises."

Nolla was wrong about that. "She will. Everly's condo has been empty since she moved into the house her grandparents built." I lifted my shoulders in a half-hearted motion. "And if it doesn't work out, I'll be okay on my own. It's Hawaii after all, and lots of people live on the beach."

The color drained from Aunt Nolla's face. She grabbed my shoulders in a fierce grip and shook. "Don't you be living like a bum, young lady. You come right back here where you belong if—"

"I was teasing," I said, shrugging out of her grasp. "Everly signed the condo over to me, and I have the deed right here in my bag. It'll be fine." But I wasn't sure it would be. I'd reached my cousin's voice mail the last few times I called, and she hadn't so much as texted me back. I should have postponed the trip, but my stubborn independent streak had taken control of my common sense.

Aunt Nolla ran her palm over my crown, then cupped my cheek. "There's enough hidden red in all that dark hair for you to be a Scot like your father. It shows in your personality as well, and in those dark blue eyes. You have the best of both your parents, and they had plenty of strength, intelligence, and determination to pass on to you, even if it was perverted later. Don't you be forgetting it, Caitlin."

Tears blurred my vision. "I won't." The least I could promise her was to try and find some good in the memories of my childhood.

She nodded. "Be off with you. I expect you to ring me

up every two weeks, right then?"

That was a given. "And I'll always be available for questions and emergencies, and to keep Dobney in line. I promise."

A loud honk interrupted us. "Gotta go." I stuffed the Tarot deck into my handbag, gave her a quick hug, and wheeled my suitcase to the waiting taxi. After settling in, I twisted to watch out the back window while the streets of Torquay disappeared in the distance, my insides dancing with excitement. Tomorrow I'd be in Hawaii. Totally unlike the English Riviera where I grew up, this new ocean would be warm. Maybe I'd learn to surf.

It was my last happy thought for long while.

The stress of international travel coupled with life-changing decisions left me tired and cranky. After the taxi ride to the train station, train to the airport, and never-ending series of flights, I swore I'd never do it again. I'd made a huge mistake in selecting the least expensive travel plan, especially since Everly had offered to pay for my ticket. Bloody stubbornness was my worst fault.

Rain poured down during the cock-up of a landing in Honolulu, and didn't let up until *after* I wrangled my suitcase onto a bus heading for the North Shore. Queasy, and with my head pounding in an unnatural rhythm, was not how I'd planned to arrive in my new home. Why had I been so pigheaded as to not let Everly know my arrival date and time? Surely she would have collected me at the airport.

If I hadn't been completely out of sorts, and the variety of odors crowded into the bus weren't aggravating my churning stomach, the ride would have been delightfully entertaining. Apparently the Hawaiian population spoke a variety of Asian languages and some colorful pidgin, as well as English, and the people were as varied as their vocabulary. When the bus reached the North Shore (I recognized the view from a ton of Internet searches), I made my way up four rows of seats, and handed a paper with my new address to the bus driver. "Will you let me know when I should get off, please?"

He jerked his head in my direction, and blinked a few times. "Where you be from?"

The lilt in his voice washed over me, calmed my nerves, and soothed my nausea. I wanted to listen to him forever, but it was my turn to talk. "England by way of Ireland and Scotland. I carry a tad of all three in my accent."

He nodded, his smile bright and welcoming. "Six more stops. It's around the end of the North Shore, so you sit on down, now, so's you'll be safe."

I sat. And counted stops. At six I lugged my suitcase to the front of the bus, and the sweet driver lifted it to the ground for me. "Thanks. It's my first day and..." I had to swallow down the threat of tears. It was a curse, how kindness always brought out the waterworks. "You've really helped."

He patted my suitcase. "It'll be down the road there. The condo office'll be able to die-rect you, Miss."

I wanted to throw my arms around him and hug him tight, but controlled myself. That sort of thing wasn't done, had been beaten out of me before the age of five. But I needed something, some connection, so I settled for waving the bus off, and then braced my shoulders, and adjusted the duffle. I sucked in a breath and took a scant minute to appreciate the soft fragrances of flowers, ocean, and tropical happiness before I took a firm grip on my suitcase and faced my new life head-on.

With determination I plowed forward, suitcase wheels bouncing over bits of crushed stone that had blown across the cement. My attention zipped back and forth between the view and so many new-to-me plants and flowers. I wasn't paying any mind to the path, and was yanked to a sudden stop when my suitcase wheels got caught in a heavily leafed vine. I tossed my duffle aside, and hunkered down to check out the problem.

The vine had wrapped around the bar attaching the tire to the frame of my luggage so tightly I couldn't work it free. Frustrated, I stood, straddled the plant, braced my feet into the soft soil, and wrapped the loose ends of the offending vine around my hands. Three hard tugs later, the only progress I made was to dig red welts into my palms. I blew on the tender areas while I considered what to do next.

A human-shaped shadow blocked the sun. "Can I help?" His voice was warm, husky, and nice.

A moment of trepidation slithered along my nerves. Hawaii had a reputation for a high incidence of crime , and I didn't plan to be a victim. Of anything. I glanced at him, shading my eyes, but it was still too bright to see his aura. Smears of paint covered one cheek and his hands, and there was an artist's brush tucked into his shirt pocket.

If he was a con artist, or worse, I had to give him credit for unique props. And he was cute. I was a sucker for sun-kissed blond hair and... huh. Couldn't tell what color his eyes were, either. "Uh..." What had he asked me? Oh, yeah. Help. "Who are you, and do you have a machete?"

His smile was instantaneous. Made the red streaks on his face crinkle. "Jace Porter. No machete, but I can try giving that vine a tug."

Sweat had beaded on my forehead, I probably smelled like dirty socks, and my travel clothes were rumpled beyond repair. I gave it a mental shrug since there wasn't a darn thing I could do about my appearance or eau de travel. "I'd be grateful for your help."

I pointed at the easel sitting several yards to our left. "Does painting require the use of any sharp implements?"

"Not really." He tipped his head to the side. "How about I try brute strength, and we'll go from there?"

I stepped aside, making a swooping gesture with my arm. "Please. I could just leave it, but...it's all I have." Oh, pisser. I sounded pathetic.

Jace bent over my suitcase, moving the wheel this way and that. "Where are you from? I like the accent."

I couldn't think of any reason not to tell him. "Torquay. It's on the English Riviera."

He twisted to look up at me. "Didn't know there was a Riviera in England. Is it warm? Like here?"

"Nice in the summer, but usually not as hot as it is today." I swiped at the sweat trailing down my face.

"You'll adjust to Hawaiian climate in no time. Cooler clothes and some slippahs will help." He stood, holding up the end of the vine. "Got it."

The tension that had been building in my temples released. "Thanks. You've helped me avoid a full-on migraine."

"Welcome." Jace snagged the strap on my duffle, and handed it to me. "Want some help with the suitcase?"

Heat bathed my cheeks. "No, thanks anyway, but I can get it." I quickly grabbed the handle on my suitcase to prevent any additional offers of help. "Oh, what are slippahs?"

He pointed to his feet. "Flip-flops to non-Hawaiians."

"Of course. I should have guessed that. Thanks for your help, Jace." I turned, hurrying toward the housing office.

"Wait," he called. "What's your name?"

I twisted around for a second, smiled, and waved. But I wasn't about to tell him my name. Americans were so quick to share personal particulars, it was a bit unnerving, and not the Brit way at all. Jace watched me walk away. I could sense his gaze between my shoulder blades, and couldn't decide if it was nice or not. Probably nice, but a girl couldn't be too careful.

A few minutes later I pushed into the air-conditioned building the bus driver had pointed out, and immediately heaved a sigh of relief. The cool air chilled my overheated skin, and I shivered. It would definitely take my body a few weeks to adjust to the difference in temperature. I tossed the unruly strands of my long hair back, and headed for the door marked *Office*. At least the signs were direct and to the point.

The woman behind the desk was the first nondescript person I'd seen since arriving in Hawaii. After spotting so many colorful personalities, it rattled me to meet a woman with mouse brown hair, dull eyes, pasty complexion, and monotone voice. And worse, her name tag read, Ms. Brown. It might have been funny if I wasn't so bloody tired. And for the record, pasty skin in the Islands should be impossible. It was abnormal.

Ms. Brown looked over my deed, and, without so much as a quirk of a smile, held up a ring of keys. "Ms. Gray left these for you. They're all the same except these two." She pointed to a smallish silver one and an odd-shaped gold one. "The silver one lets you into the swimming pool gate, and the gold one opens your mailbox. Welcome to your new home, Ms. Connor. I'm sure Ms. Gray left you a copy of the rules and regulations of our community. If not, check back with me and I'll see to it." She dropped the keys into my hand, and turned back to her computer before I could nod my thanks.

So much for friendly management. It was a blessing I'd met the bus driver and Jace first, or my welcome to the Islands would have been less than hospitable.

I made my way along the twisting sidewalk, tugging my heavier-by-the-minute suitcase, and longed for a pair of shorts, a t-shirt, and some flip-flops. The condo units were individual, joined by a series of sidewalks that provided a lot of privacy, but were close enough to neighbors if a person wanted to be friendly. I followed the numbered signs until I reached my new address, stopped, and stared at the front porch. Big, partially covered patio, amazing view of the ocean, and an open slider leading to the bedroom. Sheer curtains lifted in the breeze, drifted out the door, and caught on the siding for a second before fluttering back into place. They moved with every fresh gust of air.

My slider was *open*.

I checked the house number against the deed. Right house.

My new home was unlocked.

Panic zinged my nerves. I clenched the keys in my fist so tight the metal bit into my palm.

One breath. Six. It had to be Everly. Aunt Nolla must have called her and warned her I was arriving earlier than expected. I'd read several articles about the high crime rate in the Islands, but...

A shadow moved between the window and the bed.

My insides knotted.

Male. Not Everly.

Chapter 2

PAGE OF SWORDS

Important news coming your way.
Prepare to hear the truth.

RUN! THE PRIMAL COMMAND BELLOWED FROM DEEP in my brain. I dug my heels in, fighting the urgent demand, and slapped my hand over my mouth to stop the scream clawing up my throat.

Public place. Safe. *My* home. Not gonna run.

The front door opened, and a grungy old man stepped onto the patio. "Aloha, Caitlin."

His voice was whisper soft, but carried over the sound of the waves. Slightly unnerving. Still, I could take him if necessary. I gave myself a mental kick. How ridiculous to consider attacking an old man. I tried to scan his aura, but the adrenaline crashing through me screwed up my witchy senses.

"Bloody hell." A chill of recognition rippled through my entire body, and the world went blank for a second. Or maybe longer. No. My eyes were closed. I cranked them open and stared. Sure enough, he was an exact replica of the guy who sold me my ancient deck of Tarot cards.

This old man's smile was serene. The antique shop

proprietor never smiled. And maybe the eyes were off, not sitting quite the same on his face.

My nerves hiked up a notch. This entire scene was impossible. One man had been a fixture in Torquay all my life, not that I'd ever entered his shop until the day my shoelace broke outside the door. And *this* old man was acting like he lived *here*. I squinted, taking in the details of his face. Doppelganger for sure.

But wait, I flew here, so no reason he couldn't as well. But that was crazy. The one and only time we talked was when I purchased my Tarot deck. Maybe my memory was off. Had to be, because why would he be stalking *me*? Besides, no one strolled out of a house they didn't own wearing shorts that showed off ancient, knobby knees...unless they'd gone 'round the bend.

Bloody hell, I never should have devoured that thriller on the flight. It was messing me up as badly as my parents had.

He moved toward me, looking all normal and peaceful. "I'm Kahuna Aukele, Everly Gray's maternal grandfather."

I automatically reached in the front pocket of my jeans for my mobile, but yanked out a few dollar bills instead. I'd exchanged my pounds for American money at the airport, and left my cell phone for Aunt Nolla 'cause it wouldn't work here anyway. Now things had gone completely arseways, and there was no way I could double-check this guy's creds with Everly. Time to suck it up. I tipped my chin up and glared at him. "Can you prove you're related? And how did you get in my house?" I dangled the key ring in front of him.

Gnarled hands came together like he was praying, and then he bowed. "Namasté, Caitlin, all is well." He straightened, and with a nimble move, reached his hand behind his waist.

A gun. Was this old guy gonna *shoot* me? Should I blast him with magic? Nope. Might accidently kill him, and wouldn't *that* be a bloody mess if he really was related to Everly. I backpedaled in double time, tripped over my suitcase, and landed arse over tit. Pain shot through my ankle. "Damn it." Exhaustion and the psychic thriller I'd read had taken a serious toll on my sanity, and now I had to hobble around on my first day in Hawaii with a twisted ankle. It was totally unacceptable.

He rushed toward me, faster than knobby knees should be able to move. A photograph flapped in his hand. "Are you hurt, young Caitlin?"

I must have nodded, but my attention was on the picture of Everly and Pierce holding hands. The old guy was wrapping silky cords around their wrists. It had to be a photograph of their handfasting. I stared at the old man. Brown eyes filled with concern looked back at me.

"You're real." Pisser. There was a nasty wobble in my words.

"Most of the time, yes." He used his free hand to help me up, supporting both me and my duffle, and then he handed me the photograph. "Will this do as proof of my identity?"

I balanced on my good foot, and traced my finger over the picture. "Yes. But how, and why did you follow me from Torquay? Why didn't you tell me you were related to

Everly when I bought my Tarot cards?"

He cocked his head. "It was necessary to get them into your hands. The shop proprietor was kind enough to allow me access to his establishment for a short time, but I'm not stalking you, young Caitlin. Simply following my life path wherever and however it leads me."

He couldn't be serious. "You flew to England to set up my..." I rubbed the outline of my Tarot cards against the fabric of the duffle with my free hand, then stared at Au...something. Whatever his name was, if he lied to me I wanted to catch him. "And then you boogied back here to break into my new home?" Yep. Anger and panic rocked my voice. Anger because I didn't like surprises. And panic because I'd spotted wisps of magic floating around him. The love-hate relationship I had with my Wiccan heritage messed with my emotions something fierce. It had become debilitating.

He nodded. "Yes. It was necessary. Your other grandparents have passed beyond the veil, and the trip would have been more difficult for them. I am what some might label your Godfather, and guiding you on your path is my duty."

Duty. Right. I needed to run this by Everly, but it probably wasn't urgent, seeing as this guy obviously had no intention of hurting me. Best to play along and see what he was up to. I glanced at the photograph. "Wish I could have been here for the ceremony." Everly and Pierce were barefoot, and wearing just-kissed expressions. Sandy toes and salty kisses. I wanted what they shared *so* bad. But later. When I was old like them.

The guy...Kahuna something, had righted my suitcase. "What was your name again?" I asked.

"Aukele. Let's get you inside." One of his hands gripped my elbow, the other my suitcase handle, and he tugged us both toward the house as quickly as I could hop.

He hummed deep in his throat before he spoke. "There's fresh juice, and I'll need to mend your injury."

Say what? "Are you a doctor?"

"A healer."

Memories flashed through my mind—Everly healing Pierce back in Ireland, and me working with her to mirror, and then blast, my mother's killing energy right back at her. I shuddered. A huge part of the reason I'd left England was to get away from *that* memory, and here it was, up front and bloody nasty. "A healer like Everly?"

He pushed the front door open. "Yes. We share the gift."

I braced against the doorframe while Aukele wheeled my suitcase inside, and then hopped after him, taking in my new home. One big room with an overstuffed sofa and chair, bamboo floors, and off to the side a sparkling clean kitchen. A prickle of tears stung my eyes. Everly *gave* me this condo. I'd be forever grateful, and would somehow find a way to pay her back. I was home. I flopped into a corner of the sofa, closed my eyes, and inhaled the mixed scent of pineapple and some kind of exotic flower. "I'm not like Fion Connor."

Kahuna Aukele brushed his hand over the top of my head, and an incredible sense of calm spread through me. "No, you're not. You've chosen wisely, Caitlin."

The calm fled, and my eyelids popped open. "What?"

Those damned all-knowing, well-traveled eyes looked right through me. "To honor the Wiccan gifts you've inherited, and to use the Tarot for...justice. I'm here, Caitlin to forewarn you. Your gift is not in reading the cards, but in using your Wiccan heritage to ensure the truth is upheld. You carry the gift of justice."

Bloody hell, but he was a nutters old man, for sure. I immediately corrected him. "Being a witch fits me 'cause I'm all about doing no harm, but I'll just be *reading* the cards. No judgment or justice attached. It's important to honor free will and all." And I was not going to become a *practicing* witch, not with my unpredictable mutant DNA.

Aukele didn't answer me, just turned and strolled into the kitchen.

The underlying concern that had been riding me since I made the decision to move struck full force. On my own in a new country, not much cushion in the way of money, no job in sight, and, as Aunt Nolla kept reminding me, Tarot reading wasn't a high-paying profession. Was even illegal in some places. But I had a home and a cousin I absolutely adored.

And the cards kept telling me it was the right thing to do. Between the Ace of Wands recommending self-reliance, spiritual strength, and confidence, and the Ten of Pentacles suggesting a blessed and sacred heritage reaching into the past and future, there was no choice but to honor the message. Not when those two cards repeatedly showed up in my daily practice spreads two or three times every week...for the past four months.

It wasn't a coincidence.

I slid a look into the kitchen area. Surely Everly's grandfather wasn't capable of manipulating which cards came up in my daily reading, was he?

Aukele made his way to the sofa, and put a napkin and tall glass of pineapple juice within reach on the coffee table. "I'll leave you to get settled."

He did some kind of disappearing act. I stared at the space where he'd been standing for a long time. Maybe he didn't need an airplane to travel across oceans and continents. Maybe he teleported. I shook my head. Sleep deprivation made me seriously loopy. I swallowed the last of my juice, stood, and headed for the loo. I was halfway across the great room when it hit me. No pain. Full range of motion in my ankle. Damn. He *had* healed me.

And now I was in debt to a crazy, magical man who made mincemeat of normalcy.

HOT AND SWEATY, I STARTLED awake, heart pounding. It took me a minute to remember where I was. Hawaii. Aukele. Pineapple juice, a delicious bowl of fresh fruit waiting for me in the kitchen, and then exhausted sleep.

Sunlight drenched the bedroom in bright heat, and my mouth tasted bitter-dry. I reached for my watch. I'd slept for almost twenty-four hours. I kicked free of the covers, and headed to the bathroom for a much-needed cool shower. To my delight, Everly had stocked the bath with a selection of feminine soaps, shampoos, and lotions, making it impossible to choose just one. I shut my eyes, scooped a bottle off the shelf, then stepped under the spray and lathered up. A delightful, sparkling scent of citrus surrounded me, so I lathered up again, absorbing the fragrance and rubbing the stiffness from my arms and legs. It was time well spent, and worth starting the day later than I'd planned.

The hollow ache in my stomach reminded me I'd barely managed to eat some of the fruit before tumbling into bed. And unpacking had been out of the question. With a sigh, I dumped the contents of my suitcase onto the bed. There was nothing for it but to grab shorts, a t-shirt, and some underwear from the wadded-up mess of clothes. I dressed in record time, a mix of anticipation and excitement scrambling for attention, but one thing was absolutely clear: I wanted to make a mark on my new city. No, that wasn't right. Village? Town? The North Shore simply didn't fit any normal description, so I shrugged off my urge to define it.

There was one more thing I needed to do before I left for the day. I carefully removed my grimoire, athame, pentacle, and chalice from my duffle, and placed them on the dresser. Just because it wasn't safe for me to practice witchcraft didn't stop me from honoring the Craft. The dresser would do as a makeshift altar, but later I'd set up a proper, respectful place for them. That done, I filled my small handbag with money, passport and Tarot cards, then slipped it over my shoulder. That done, I swung by the kitchen to gulp another glass of pineapple juice, and stepped into a pair of flip-flops. Ah...what did that guy say? Oh. Slippahs. Time to explore my new neighborhood.

The crash of powerful waves, a gentle breeze, and

speckled sunlight dancing through leaves greeted me. With a grin, I nudged my sunglasses into place and went in search of food. Ten minutes or so passed before I reached a grouping of shops that included a Starbucks.

When I pushed the door open, a blast of coffee-scented air greeted me. Apparently it was a unique aroma intrinsic to every Starbucks, because I could've sworn I was back home in the Torquay store. With several deep breaths I inhaled the rich fragrance, letting its familiarity erase any trace of homesickness before it had a chance to take root.

I glanced at the barista's name tag. "Good morning, Alana," I said, pointing to the pastries. "I've never seen oatcakes at Starbucks before. They look a lot like Irish scones, dense and rich."

"They're only sold on Island. Very good and filling. You'll need a drink, yah?"

"Yes, please. One oatcake and a *venti* Chai latte."

When my order was ready, I thanked Alana and wandered outside for a lazy walk along the storefronts, to explore my new neighborhood and savor my breakfast. Until I came to the Ola Boutique. Yeah, the window was staged with clothes that made me want to spend money, but more importantly, the store had...presence. "I wonder what Ola means?" I mumbled the question around a bite of oatcake.

"Life."

I jumped, spilling a huge splat of latte down the front of my t-shirt, then spun to face the voice. The single syllable she'd spoken had feathered over my skin, leaving tiny chill bumps behind.

"Sorry. I didn't mean to startle you, but I thought you saw me in the window." She pointed at our reflections mirrored in the plate glass. "I'm Hannah Matthews, and Ola is my creation."

"Ah." Excellent. Not only had my chest been slightly singed with hot liquid, now turned cool, but I'd lost my ability to speak. While I swallowed my last bite of oatcake, I opened my witchy sight, scanning her. Gold. And a lacy, fog-like shroud of protection I'd never seen before. It gave me pause, but the gold was vibrant, and since I wasn't getting any warning signs, I plunged in with both feet. "You're tall. And golden."

Her light, crisp laughter filled the space around us. "It's the sunshine," she said, reaching around me to unlock the shop door. "Come in and keep me company while I get things set up for the day."

There was something about her eyes. Gray, no, more like warm, molten silver. If anyone asked, I'd say this woman had seen even more *life* than Everly and I combined. And after my cousin and I eliminated my wicked bitch of a mother, it was a tough call for anyone to match the pain hiding behind our eyes. I hadn't been able to look into a mirror, to hold my own gaze, for more than a few seconds since that day. It hurt too bloody much.

Hannah pointed toward an overstuffed chair patterned with tropical flowers. "Sit and tell me all about your fascinating accent, and how you ended up having oatcakes and chai on the most beautiful beach in the world."

I needed to find some normal, conversational words. "I grew up on the English Riviera, Torquay area, and my cousin lives—used to live—here in North Shore. She moved to Manoa, so her condo became my new home." Everly's generosity still blew me away.

Hannah busied herself preparing a deep tub with ice and several bottles of fruit juice. "And now you have a new ocean to explore..." She let the last word hang.

"Oh, I'm sorry. What a tosser I am not to introduce myself. My name's Caitlin Connor, but you can call me Cait."

She glanced at me, assessing. "Nice to meet you, Cait. Ola is a gathering place for women. There are clothes and jewelry, of course, because we girls need something to keep our hands busy while we work out the kinks in our lives. More important are the art, words, and friendship that are here to nourish our emotions. But mostly this is a place where women seek peace for their souls, where questions are asked and answered."

My insides chilled. There was something familiar about her tone, something making my witchy senses hum with interest. I stood and crumpled the empty oatcake sack, then downed a huge gulp of rapidly cooling latte. "Lovely shop and all, but I'd best be getting on with my day. Nice to meet you, Hannah."

I didn't make it to the door before her voice wrapped around me. "We witches recognize our own kind, Caitlin."

Chapter 3

EIGHT OF SWORDS

Trapped. Powerless.

I RAN, BLINDLY TOSSING MY HALF-FULL CUP AND paper bag at a trash can as I rounded the corner to circle behind the shops, away from the car park, people, and reality. I desperately needed quiet and space to think. Hannah admitted to being a witch. Out loud and to a stranger. Why hadn't I recognized her? And then it hit me. My own witchy, inside-out energy had responded to her, and warned me by lowering my body temperature. It made sense that witches without my kind of mutant DNA had a layer of protection over their aura.

The sound of my flip-flops slapping against the pavement mingled with a distinctive, squeaky rhythm of sneakers, and with the frantic beat of my heart. Surely Hannah wouldn't chase me down. I glanced over my shoulder. Didn't see anyone, but the footsteps sounded closer. Where were they coming from?

I pushed harder, faster.

And tripped, my knees and palms scraping the rough surface of the alleyway. "Bloody hell, that hurts!"

Still no one behind me. Could the footsteps have come from the other side of the bushes lining the alley? I seriously needed to stop reading about the crime rates in Hawaii. And definitely no more psychic thrillers. Ever.

I looked down.

Man's shoe.

Bloody.

I turned my head, eyeing a trail of red-brown spatter that led from the shoe to its mate...and to an unnaturally crumpled body that rested in a huge puddle of blood. Too much blood. The scream started in my gut, worked its way out, and didn't stop until Hannah's trembling hand closed over my shoulder. "Did you see what happened? Are you hurt?" she asked.

Words stuck in my throat, so I shook my head, and pointed toward the body. "Dead?"

"Has to be with those unnaturally staring eyes. I'm not going to check, because I don't have a clue how to help him, and I'd only contaminate the crime scene." Hannah's phone was in her hand, and she punched in some numbers. "I'm calling nine-one-one."

I shoved awkwardly to my feet, and brushed the grit from my knees and palms. Anything to keep from looking at the dead body. My breakfast oatcake threatened to reappear, and I swallowed hard, turning my attention to Hannah.

Her voice was taut with more than shock. She was scared. My brain kicked in, and I listened to what she was saying to the emergency dispatcher. This was *her* shop. Bloody hell, I'd stumbled into a witch's den complete with dead bodies. Not at all what I had in mind when I decided to embrace a somewhat-Wiccan lifestyle.

I would have made a fast exit, except I'd been around enough cops to know they'd track me down. I was, after all, the lucky sucker who had tripped over the dead guy's shoe. They'd have questions. I didn't have answers. It was a bad scene, one requiring backup. I started to dig in my handbag for my nonexistent mobile. That needed to be fixed first thing.

Hannah tucked her phone in her pocket, and narrowed her eyes. "Did you see anyone?"

"No. I wasn't looking, just running. Were you chasing me?"

Her eyes widened. "No. I'd just stepped outside to turn the open sign over when I heard you scream, and ran to see what happened. There was no one else around."

Confused, I glanced at her feet. Ballet slippers. "Sorry, I'm sure I heard footsteps." I shrugged, trying to control the tremors threatening to take over. "Do you recognize him? The body is right next to your back door." I gestured toward the Ola Boutique lettering on a solid wood door.

"It's just my storage and delivery area, and doesn't connect to the inside of the shop. Thank the goddesses you saw me earlier, or they'd be trying to accuse me of killing him."

I blinked at her. "Did you kill him?"

Hannah frowned.

"Shit." What was the matter with me, to have asked her that?

Her frown deepened into a scowl.

Not sure if it was my question or the curse word irritating her, I attempted a save. "Shitiski."

Her frown relaxed. "No, I didn't kill him...although..."

Although? I backed away from her. Maybe a quick getaway was my best option after all. I could go straight to the police station to give them my statement. Except I didn't know where it was. And the sirens blasting in the distance held me frozen in place.

The situation with Fion Connor's death taught me a lot about how to effectively deal with the Metropolitan Police, but back then I had Everly and Pierce for backup. Still, these cops probably weren't much different, which meant it was going to be a long day.

Within minutes the alley entrance was blockaded by three patrol cars, and there was an unmarked closing in fast. Showtime. I aimed a sideways glance at Hannah, and confirmed what I expected: white face, quivering lips, and terrified eyes. But after she gave the body a long stare, she released a sigh that held the distinct sensation of relief. It raised the hair on my arms.

"You have two seconds to tell me what he did to you, Hannah."

She whipped around to face me. "Threatening me for months. Wanted me to use the Craft for harm. Please tell them you saw me in the shop. I didn't do this, Cait." Her voice was thick and tight with fear.

"Promise me you didn't kill him?" No harm on double-checking, especially with the *although* she'd tacked on to her first denial.

Hannah took a deep breath, exhaled, and held my

gaze. "Promise. But I won't deny I'm glad he's dead."

I fingered the Tarot deck in my handbag. I would rather have done a reading to get to the truth of it straightaway, but we were out of time. Four uniformed coppers climbed out of the squad cars, took one look at the scene, and conferred for a second. A female officer approached the body, and two others, both male, circled to the rear of their cars.

The single remaining officer strode toward us, wearing his serious cop face.

I rolled my shoulders back, preparing for the worst. The two officers who'd circled behind their vehicles were in the process of covering their street clothes with overalls, paper shoes, facemasks, and gloves. I shivered. My DNA was all over the crime scene. And so was Hannah's.

Between her golden aura and my intuition, I was fairly certain she didn't kill the guy, so I'd do what I could to protect her. Being a murderess myself helped put this sort of thing in perspective, not that I'd help her out if she *was* guilty, but I was almost positive she wasn't. My dense, inside-out energy had a different hum when it recognized its own kind, deeper and slower. The sensation startled me. Why hadn't I noticed it when I first met Hannah? I should have known right off she was Wiccan, but that lacy pattern covering her aura had thrown me. I made a mental note to pay better attention, and scanned the scene in front of me. This was a bloody inconvenient way to start my new life, but it helped clarify the reason for Kahuna Aukele's visit yesterday. Crafty old man must be clairvoyant. I'd have to check with Everly...soon as I got myself out of this mess.

I brushed at the grit embedded in my hands. They stung like crazy, and so did my knees. I wasn't complaining, not with a corpse sprawled a few yards away. He'd have probably been happier than hell to trade places with me.

I copped a glance at Hannah. She was rigid, looked like she was ready to splinter into a dozen pieces, and was definitely hiding something. I made a snap decision to back up her claim of innocence.

As the policeman approached us, he backed us farther from the corpse. "I'm Officer Fields, Honolulu Police," he said, and showed his identification. He had an iPad in hand and typed in our particulars. Another officer joined us, introduced herself, and moved Hannah to a different area. The tension and fear radiating from Hannah was palpable, so I silently willed her to do some deep breathing. Facing a police interrogation goes much better when you have your wits about you.

Fields asked me to describe what happened. No surprise there. I managed to give a creditable outline of the bare facts, during which an officer—tall, sandy hair with blond highlights, well-built, and with a three-bar chevron on his sleeve—donned protective gear before he entered the cordoned-off area. He had the look of a homicide detective. When he backed away from the body and stripped off his protective gear, Fields wrapped up his questions.

The tall, sandy-haired copper had a no-nonsense, command attitude that left no doubt I was in trouble. He would've fit right in with the Metropolitan Police. And there was something else...something familiar about him. It messed my head up something fierce.

His green-eyed glare bored into me when he flashed his badge. I glanced at the gold shield, stalling for time since I still hadn't decided exactly what to say about Hannah. He flipped the ID back into his pocket. "I'm Detective Adam Stone, Ms. Connor. We weren't expecting you until next week."

Say what? The calm façade I'd been struggling to maintain shattered, and there went the damn oatcake, churning around in my stomach again. "How do you know who I am?"

"Everly Gray is a good friend, and I believe you've met my sister."

I snapped my fingers as everything fell into place. "Annie. You look just like her."

A man climbed out of Stone's car, and, after a quick nod to the detective, headed our way. Recognition and confusion exploded in my brain, and his easy stride confirmed my reaction. "Jace Porter?"

Detective Stone's eyebrows hiked. "You know Officer Porter?"

Jace shoved his hand in front of Stone, offering it to me. "We met yesterday, but I didn't catch her name."

There was no help for it. I clasped his hand, and gave it a firm shake. "Caitlin Connor, Officer Porter."

Desperately, I tried to piece a pile of facts into a coherent picture. Police officer who dabbled in art, or an artist who paid the bills with his law enforcement salary?

He wasn't wearing a uniform, but his khaki pants and white shirt didn't diminish his air of authority one whit. Jace's gaze latched onto me and didn't waver. Brown eyes—no, green. I blinked. Blue? Whatever color they were, they sucked me in and held on tight.

"But you're an artist." I blurted the words before I could curb my tongue.

His smile broadened, and I spotted a fleeting dimple, like a cheek wink. "Forensic artist, Ms. Connor."

A forensic artist who dabbled with red paint. Questions tumbled through my mind. "But—"

Detective Stone tipped his head toward the unmarked vehicle. "Let's sit inside."

The sun had been beating on my head for a while now, so I was right with him on that plan. "Guess you told Everly I'm here?"

He shook his head. "Any reason you haven't contacted her?"

"I, um, I'm stubborn to a fault and wanted to make it these first few days on my own."

"Must be genetic," he said, blowing out a sigh.

What a pisser. He probably knew all about Everly and me killing Fion, which *might* put me in the hot seat for this guy's murder. I licked the dryness from my lips. "Genetic?" I croaked, and cleared my throat to try again. "What do you mean by genetic, Detective Stone?"

He opened the back door of his sedan, and motioned me inside. "Everly and stubborn. Can't separate them, but her curiosity is the killer." He narrowed his gaze on me. "Just my luck that particular trait is probably genetic in your family as well."

I sat on the back seat, swung my legs inside, and breathed in the stale scent from the air conditioner. Stone closed the car door and circled around the back of the sedan. Officer Porter took the shotgun seat, opened the computer attached to the console, and poised his fingers over the keypad.

I shook my finger at the computer. "That's not art."

"I'm versatile." He shot me that infectious smile again.

Detective Stone slid into the back seat next to me. That had to be against protocol, and I must have looked shocked, because he shook his head. "Talk to me, Cait. What happened here?"

My tongue stuck to the roof of my mouth, and it took a second to work it free. The only thing in my head was a vivid image of the dead guy, blood, and wide-open, staring eyes. "I tripped over his shoe. Was running because..." I paused, glancing at Hannah through the car windshield.

He pointed at my feet. "Slippahs not sneakers. Why were you running?"

I followed his finger, and wiggled my toes, the shimmer of purple polish sparkling in a ray of sunlight. The pedicure was intended to be a "new start" gift to myself just before I left Torquay, but now the happy color mocked my optimism. I shifted my gaze to meet Detective Stone's icy stare.

The cool air in the car seeped through my damp t-shirt, and I shivered. Startled, I brushed my hands over my forehead, and around the back of my neck. Sweaty. When had that happened? Coupled with the scrapes on my knees and hands, and the coffee spill down the front of my shirt, I looked like I'd been struggling with someone. Panic shot through me. "I didn't kill him. I was running because Hannah..."

Chapter 4

TWO OF WANDS (REVERSED)

Re-group with a new strategy.

THE RAGGED SOUND OF MY LABORED BREATHING filled the police car, and mingled with the steady clicking of Officer Porter's fingers on the keyboard.

"Hannah?" Detective Stone's voice cut into me.

My body twitched, but I held his gaze. "Do you know her, Detective Stone?"

"Not yet."

"She..." What in the ever-loving hell was I going to say? The silence weighed on my shoulders. Jace would never smile at me again after he heard this. I forced an inhalation, then blew out a resigned sigh. "She said witches recognize their own kind."

Stone's forehead knitted into tight creases. "Witches?"

I fought for control, and tossed in some attitude. "Surely you're familiar with Everly's ESP fingers and healing gifts. It shouldn't be difficult for you to accept there are witches in the world as well." I waited a beat. "Annie didn't have a problem with it." I immediately regretted voicing the reference to Stone's sister. She'd been there, had witnessed me actively using magic.

He shrugged. "Why did you run from Ms...?"

Officer Porter filled in the pause. "Hannah Matthews, sir."

Stone nodded. "Why did you run from her, Ms. Connor?"

The back of my t-shirt clung to my skin, and began to itch. I shifted, trying to pull away from the fabric. "I'm not comfortable with my paranormal gifts, Detective. I'm still trying to figure out where and how they fit in my life."

Detective Stone nodded. "Uh-huh. Did you recognize the victim?"

"No." It came out too loud, too intense, and way too scared. I couldn't stop the babble escaping my mouth. "I just got to Hawaii. I don't know anybody. Haven't seen anyone but the bus driver, the condo woman, Kahuna Aukele, Alana, and Hannah. Oh, and Officer Porter."

"That's six people, Ms. Connor, and doesn't include the other passengers on the bus." His voice was clipped.

I rubbed my palm over the bulge of the Tarot deck in my handbag. "I've never seen the victim before this morning, Detective."

"Noted. Who is Alana?"

"The barista at Starbucks. She waited on me this morning, and can verify what time I was there. Wait, so can I." I bolted from the car, ran toward the trashcan, and dug until I found my crumpled bag. There must be a time stamp on it. Had to be.

I turned—still rummaging through the Starbucks bag—and did a full-body bump into Officer Porter. Chills swept through me. Good ones, not magic ones. The kind that took my breath and made me want to snuggle closer. "Ah, sorry. I didn't realize..." I skipped back a step, meeting his blue...make that green-eyed stare.

"Detective Stone is with the crime scene unit." That husky voice was smooth enough to make a woman dip in and stay a while.

I shook free of his gaze, and sidled away. Surely I couldn't be attracted to him. An artist, yes. A cop, no. Heat flashed in my cheeks, and I stuck my nose into the bag, heaving a sigh of relief when I spotted the wadded up receipt. I dug it out, and handing it to him, I pointed to the time stamp. "See here, I was in the coffee shop."

Porter shook his head, pulled a plastic baggie from his pocket, and motioned for me to drop the receipt inside.

There was something about his closed expression that sent a trickle of warning along my spine. "What aren't you telling me?" I scanned the area, spotted Detective Stone talking to Hannah, and a tall man closing the door on a white truck labeled with bright blue letters: MEDICAL EXAMINER. I wheeled to face Porter. "You don't know the time of death yet, so my receipt is meaningless."

Porter cocked his head. "You seem familiar with homicide investigations, Ms. Connor. Why is that?" There was no threat in his tone, but he definitely expected an answer.

I clamped my lips shut. According to the autopsy report, Fion Connor died of heart failure, which was about as close to the truth as anyone could legally describe. Death by malignant energy overdose wasn't acceptable on an official report. Jace Porter's multi-colored eyes narrowed to a single, penetrating hazel stare. I held it, no blinking allowed.

"I read a lot of mysteries, Officer." Truth. It was always good to tell the cops the truth, or for damn sure they'd catch you out. I desperately wanted to ring up Everly, but my stubbornness clouded common sense. At least that's what Aunt Nolla always said, and she was right, it did get me into messes all the bloody time.

There was movement off to my right. Detective Stone had escorted Hannah to a squad car, and was gesturing for her to get in. She glanced at me, and a wave of terror shot into my chest. I rubbed at it. Had she used dark energy or light? I couldn't tell for sure, but my inside-out energy didn't respond. Surely that meant Hannah used white energy like Everly did. No matter, Hannah had sent a frantic cry for help I couldn't ignore, at least not yet. I needed facts.

After the car holding Hannah sped away, Stone made his way back toward Officer Porter and me.

A niggling thought screamed for attention. *The cards. You're the oracle of justice.* I shoved at the thought, and glared at Porter. "Surely you're not arresting Hannah?"

"Detective Stone's call, Caitlin." He sounded firm, dutiful even, but there was doubt lurking in those mysterious eyes. And my name had rolled off his tongue like he savored the feel of it. It knocked me off my game, but only for a second.

I spun to face Stone. "You arrested Hannah?"

He tensed, tapped Jace on the shoulder, and drew him

a few feet away from me. It was one of those moments I'd come to hate, when using my inside-out energy could result in enough benefit to be worth the risk of potentially causing harm. I touched the edge, hoping I only needed to skim the surface. Not enough. I dipped in, just breaking the outer layer, and spread the energy to encompass Stone and Jace so I could listen.

"We have photographs, but since his face is so cut up, I want you to make a sketch we can use to canvas. Do your best filling in his facial features. Matthews admits he frequented her shop, tried to buy a curse from her, but she denies knowing his name. ME got prints, but I want more than a name on him. I'm damn sure she knows the guy, and I want proof. Today."

"On it." Porter jogged toward the body, and I attempted to arrange my face into an I-heard-nothing blank surface.

Stone didn't buy it. "Time for us to continue our chat, Ms. Connor." He took my elbow in a firm grasp, led me toward his car, helped me into the back, and took the driver's seat for himself. "Start at the beginning and walk me through it again. Focus on your interaction with Ms. Matthews, and anything relevant to my conversation with Porter you apparently overheard."

Oh, shi...shitiski. "How did you—?"

"Your lips moved, repeating everything I said. Start with when you arrived on island."

The man could lip-read. Out of the corner of his eye. Damn all multi-talented detectives. I closed my eyes, organized my memory, and recounted everything that had happened since the plane landed, only skipping over Hannah's confession. Detective Stone typed while I talked, his fingers slower on the keys than Officer Porter, like he was thinking while he entered my statement.

He pushed away from the computer and sighed. "What're you hiding, Caitlin?"

"Nothing. I want to make a phone call."

Detective Stone shook his head, and offered me his cell phone. "You can call, but Everly and Pierce are out of town on business. Aren't due back until the middle of next week."

I squinted at him. "How do know what I'm thinking? Are you psychic?"

"Cop intuition." He gave me a lopsided smile. "If Everly was in town, I'd have called her in to touch you before now."

"Nope. You wouldn't, because you're a by-the-book-cop, and ESP isn't admissible in court." At least it wasn't in England.

"Everly has taught me how to work around that."

The creepie-crawlies tingled under my skin. "I can ring up your sister. Annie will vouch for me." At least I hoped she would.

A shadow crossed his face. "I can't stop you from calling her, but I'll ask you not to. She's in the last three months of a difficult pregnancy, and is on complete bed rest."

Panic knotted in my chest, but no way would I enlist Annie's help, not when she had...issues. Which left me with one week to figure out what was going on with

Hannah and the dead guy before Everly got home and unleashed her ESP fingers on me. Did withholding information count as aiding and abetting? Bloody hell. My first morning in Hawaii and I was a criminal...by omission.

Chapter 5

Be aware of competition, not afraid of it.
Spirited debating – give it your all.

WHEN DETECTIVE STONE FINISHED GRILLING ME, I headed straight for Hannah's shop. I had questions, and damn well wanted answers. Stone had hammered at me for over an hour until I'd repeated everything I remembered from the time I left the house until I listened in on his conversation with Officer Porter. I was sick to death of the details, and needed a loo and food, plus maybe a glass of beer.

I hustled to the front of the shopping area, then took my time strolling along the walkway while I kept an eye on the front door of Ola Boutique. No one tried the doorknob, or even peered into the windows. A twinge of warning seeped into my mind. Weren't Americans notoriously curious? Then again, the crime scene was behind the shops, and not visible unless you turned the corner into the alleyway. And someone had turned the Open sign to Closed. That could account for it.

Twisting one way, then another to stretch my muscles, I surreptitiously checked out the entire area. Everyone must have been ogled out, because not a single gawker remained. I figured Hannah was still being held for questioning, but I hadn't noticed any of the officers around the front of the boutique, so it must not have been included in the crime scene. At least not yet.

I had zip experience with illegal entry, so I needed to plan my next move carefully, especially since finding the body made me a person of interest.

A gust of wind blew my hair across my face, and it took a minute of sputtering before I got it out of my mouth. And then I inhaled the scent of coconut and fried shrimp. It went straight to my feed-me-or-else receptors, and I spun around, hurrying toward a battered sign that read Uncle's: OTB, and underneath in parenthesis, On the Beach. I blew out a huge sigh when I spotted patio seating with a free table that provided a view of the Ola Boutique front door. It would be the perfect place to hang out while I planned my next move. Even better, the table was set for three people, which meant I'd have room for a Tarot spread. Grinning at the hostess, I pointed to the seat I wanted. "I'd really like to sit there, please. And could you point me to the loo?"

She wrinkled her nose. "It's almost lunch time and..." Her gaze trailed down to my scraped knees. "Oh, my, you must have taken quite a spill, yah? I'll set the table up for just one while you're in the restroom." She pointed behind her. "Right down the hallway there."

"Thanks," I said, with a flash of guilt for capitalizing on the injury card. "I'll wash up the scrapes and be right there." I'd forgotten about my bloody knees, but since they got me what I needed, I chalked it up to the Universe helping a girl out.

Forty minutes later, I was totally absorbed in the incredible flavor of coconut shrimp and a pint of Wailua Wheat ale. I'd fallen in love with On The Beach food after the first bite, and began planning a campaign to convince the manager I should use one of the more secluded tables to offer Tarot readings for their customers. I needed a public space, and surely renting a restaurant table wouldn't cost as much as leasing an entire shop.

Glancing at the Ola Boutique over the rim of my beer glass, I considered how to find the killer in the next twenty-four hours. I doubted Honolulu's finest would wait any longer before they formally arrested either Hannah or me, unless they'd already locked her up.

Nothing had changed at the shop, and my only alternative was to try the door. Hannah hadn't gone in to collect her purse before she was whisked away. And wasn't that odd? Surely they would have asked her for ID of some sort, or at least allowed her to close up the boutique. I hoped it meant they hadn't arrested her.

My eyelids fluttered down for a second while I savored the crisp, fresh taste of the beer, and then immediately popped open when my intuition zapped me. My swallow turned into an I-can't-breathe choke when a uniformed copper sidled up to the boutique door and disappeared inside. Furtive, so probably not on duty. Or maybe he'd been sent to secure the premises. And then it hit me. Hannah *chose* not to gather her belongings or lock the shop. Which meant she wanted someone to have access. It was a huge jump to a crazy conclusion, but it fit my plan. On the negative side it set me up as an accomplice—or worse, the killer.

Leaning toward the positive, I slapped some money on the table, smiled a thank you at my server, and strode toward the boutique. So much for doing a Tarot spread to steer me in the right direction. I was acting on pure gut instinct, and somehow it was the right thing to do. Had to be because the intuitive pull was too strong to ignore, and this dude's behavior demanded my immediate attention.

I edged up to Ola's and casually peered in the far corner of the front window. The intense sun screwed with my line of sight, but I didn't spot the guy or any movement. I strolled away from the shop to peruse the area before I barged inside, in case there was backup running a surveillance detail.

Normal sounds filled the shopping strip, and there were no visible squad cars. And wasn't that interesting, since the cop inside must have a vehicle nearby? Time to stop procrastinating and check out the situation. Squaring my shoulders, I moved to the door, turned the knob, and stepped inside.

A fragrance, lavender mixed with something light and soothing, clung to the air—and so did an undercurrent of mumbled words coming from behind a clothing display. I sucked in a breath to say something, to give him a heads-up I was in the building, but before my tongue wrapped around a syllable, he shifted from behind the display.

"Hands where I can see them. Drop your bag. Do it now." Panic put an edge on his voice, but the gun he aimed at me was rock solid steady.

I lowered my shoulder, letting my handbag slide to the floor, and raised my hands while I scanned his aura. Swirling shades of orange shifting to red at the outside edges. So good-hearted, kind, and honest, with a bent for adventure and the need to be number one. He probably wasn't going to shoot me. "Who are you? Hannah—"

He holstered his weapon. "Police. Shop's not open. You'll need to leave, Miss."

I backed up a step, and fingered a stack of t-shirts on the table next to me. There was something about the soft cotton that gave me courage. "Hannah asked me to check on things..." I let the words drift. "I don't remember you from this morning. Do you have some identification, Officer?"

"Official business. Now, move along."

I spotted the tub of melted ice, the bottles of juice floating on their sides. Yes! I plastered on my best attempt at an innocent expression. "I promised Hannah I'd see to tidying up as soon as the police were finished." Blatant lie, but I needed to slip under his attitude and hopefully find a decent guy underneath, one who'd let me poke around, and maybe even talk to me. With two long strides, I stood beside the tub, and scooped out a bottle of juice. "I need to get these in the refrigerator, and empty the water before it leaks all over the floor." To prove my point, I ran my palm under the plastic bottle, then shook the water off.

The officer fidgeted like a druggie who needed a fix. Something was way off here. I took a few steps toward him, hoping I'd spot a hall leading to a loo, or back room where there might be a sink. He backed up, bumped into the checkout counter, and glanced over his shoulder toward a bulletin board on the wall behind the register.

I followed his line of sight—straight to a photograph of him with Hannah, arms around each other, and wearing intimate smiles. Power surged through me when I realized *I* had the upper hand. "Bloody hell, you're Hannah's significant other."

Chapter 6

ACE OF SWORDS

If you find yourself in a debate,
you'll be able to make your point.

SIGNIFICANT OTHER'S WIRY FRAME DEFLATED, AND he swallowed hard. "Was. Don't know why she hasn't taken the picture down."

I pressed my toes into the soft rubber of my flip-flops, and drew in a long, calming breath. This was a one-off opportunity, and too important to mess up. "I'm Caitlin Connor. Who are you?"

"Yamoto Nori. I...we were engaged until last week. I heard the homicide announced on the scanner, and got here right after my shift ended. Expected Hannah to be here..." He clamped his lips together, and glared at me. "She's never mentioned anyone named Caitlin."

I grabbed a couple more bottles of juice, threading the long necks through my fingers, and turned toward the back of the shop. "Give me a minute to get these in the fridge."

"Hold it." His tone bit the air, and stopped me cold. "Hannah doesn't store the juice in a refrigerator. Who are you, and what the fuck are you doing here?"

I slowly turned. It was time for the truth. He'd find out anyway, since he had access to the police reports. "I met her this morning. I was here when she opened the shop, and she invited me in. I discovered the dead body right after I left. Hannah heard me scream, caught up to me, and phoned nine-one-one." I gave him my best innocent shrug. "We sort of bonded over the...incident, and I'm worried. They should be done questioning her by now. I thought maybe I could find something in here to help her."

The cop in Yamato Nori took over. "Set the bottles down."

I did, and within seconds he cuffed me. It pissed me off to the point of boiling mad, and magic exploded in my veins. I inhaled, holding the breath until my lungs burned and I got my inner witch under control. I did *not* want to blast a copper with potentially lethal energy. Damn, but I needed to learn to control the magic. It had been so volatile since Fion's death. "Look, I don't mean Hannah any harm. The opposite, in fact. She looked scared when they took her away, and witches don't abandon their own kind."

He recoiled, his olive complexion turning a putrid green. "Witch? You're one of them?"

Did I say that? Pisser. How had I ever allowed those words out of my mouth? "I seem to be, but I'm new to the Craft. Less than a year into it, actually." No point confusing him with the details about how my parents experimented with DNA-altering drugs.

His mouth twisted into a grimace. "Figures I'd bump into another one of you. It's the reason Hannah and I broke it off. I love her, but the witch crap is too much. She chose it over me, but with shit like this happening around her, I'm glad. Can't stop loving her, though. "

He thought—no, he truly believed Hannah was a murderer. "Did she know the victim? Do they have an ID on him yet?"

"Yeah. Asked around before my shift ended. Name's Ted Thatcher. Cockroach type guy. I looked into him when Hannah started having trouble, thought he might be stalking her. Turned out he was suspected of stealing ammunition from Schofield Army Barracks, and was dishonorably discharged a few years back."

Officer Nori clammed up, sudden-like.

He must have realized he'd been offering a civilian information on an ongoing case, so I hurried to reassure him. "It's all in the past. Probably doesn't pertain to his murder at all."

Panic sparked in his eyes. "I arrested Thatcher last month for breaking and entering."

And didn't that tidbit of information ring my alarm bells. "How exactly are they connected?"

Nori shifted his weight. "Thatcher broke in *here*, stalking Hannah. Later when he started hounding her for a curse, she believed he wanted it to use on me since I was the arresting officer."

And the shit got deeper. "Does Detective Stone have all this background information?" Of course he did. It was a throwaway question, but I needed time to think. The dead guy wanted Hannah, she wasn't interested, so he broke into Ola Boutique to...what? And then Yamoto Nori, aka The Ex-Fiancé, arrested Thatcher, and the Hannah-Yamoto engagement ended because he couldn't cope with her witchy ways. Bloody blue hell.

Ex-fiancé nodded, his face etched with desperation.

"You need to get out of here right now. If Detective Stone catches you messing with anything remotely connected to this crime scene, he'll..." Words failed me because I had no idea how coppers were reprimanded.

"Yeah. But I had to try and help establish an alibi for Hannah." He shoved his shoulders back, and held my gaze. "Let's go."

"Bad idea," I said, my brain humming at warp speed. "You need to leave. I need to stay because my excuse is stupid enough to be ignored, and it's very possible someone, even someone as innocent as a passerby, has noticed movement in the shop. More likely Stone has assigned regular surveillance, it being the potentially suspected killer's place of business. Better if I'm caught than you."

He hesitated. "There's an officer stationed at the crime scene tent. He won't leave his post, and since it's around the corner and down the alley, it's not likely he'll notice any activity in Ola's."

"Crime scene tent?" I asked, confused.

Yamoto cocked his head, staring at me like I'd failed moron school. "Control, preserve, record, recover, and reconstruct. Those are the rules for crime scene investigation. We have frequent afternoon rainstorms, so the investigators covered the area with a tent to protect the scene. Stone probably released you before they put it up."

Interesting stuff, and it might be useful in my new line of work—truth and justice enforcer. Yeah, I liked it. Enforcer. Sounded tough. But it wasn't the time for useless labels. "Thanks for explaining. Now let's get you out of here."

My nerves zinged. There was no reason, logical or otherwise, for me to protect Officer Yamoto Nori, except that my witchy senses were shrieking at me to hide his visit to Ola's. "I can play the dumb foreigner. You can't. Go," I said, jabbing my finger toward the door.

A car crawled past the shop. The driver was Jace Porter.

Chapter 7

EIGHT OF PENTACLES

*This is a wonderful time
to hone your skills.*

OFFICER NORI SHOOK HIS HEAD. "NOT WITHOUT YOU. Can't leave you on Hannah's property unattended."

He'd twanged my last nerve. "Jace Porter just did a surveillance drive-by, and even if he didn't spot us through the window, I'm guessing his copper intuition will nag him to double-check. You probably have all of ten seconds to slip away before he circles around and drives by the front door of Ola's again." I put some steel behind my words.

Officer Nori's face turned that sickly shade of green again. He pointed at me. "We're not done, Caitlin Eireen Connor."

He was out the door and headed for Starbucks before I realized he'd said my full name. My stomach flipped, and the tiniest bit of panic zapped my nerves. The Honolulu PD had obviously put out a bulletin with detailed information about me. Did that make me an official murder suspect?

No time to think about it. Hurriedly I threaded my

fingers through the bottles of juice and turned toward the back of the shop. Best if Jace caught me cleaning things up, as it would make my story more believable.

I'd only taken two steps before his shadow passed across the window, and there was no hesitation between the sharp rap on the door and Jace marching into Ola's like he owned the place.

I whirled to face him, letting out a startled gasp I barely had to fake. No uniform. Tan shorts, a navy t-shirt, flip-flops...ah, slippahs, and those ever-changing eyes that were boring straight into me. A knot of pain hit my chest, demanding air. I gasped again, forcing oxygen into my lungs. "You scared me." I nodded toward the door. "Thought I'd locked up."

"What are you doing here, Ms. Connor?" His posture was pure cop, but I didn't see a weapon.

"Straightening things. I didn't want Hannah to come back to a mess, especially with the melted ice." I rubbed the toe of my flip-flop over the natural wood floor. "If the bucket leaked it would ruin this gorgeous floor."

Porter sauntered toward the metal tub, glanced in, then lifted it. "Where's the sink?"

Adrenaline spun through my veins. Where the hell was the sink? "In back." Surely there was a loo back there, even if I couldn't see a likely place to dump the water...except in the flowerbeds lining the front of the boutique. "But wait. Do you mind spreading it over the plants? They could use the moisture." I sounded like a total jerk, but Porter's only reaction was raised eyebrows.

As soon as his back was turned, I fled to the rear of

the shop. Where in bloody hell did Hannah store the bottles of juice? Frantic, I scanned shelves of folded clothes, neatly arranged candles with an assortment of handcrafted glass holders, a jewelry display, and three curtained alcoves that were probably dressing rooms. Two of them faced each other across a wide hallway, but the third curtained area was set back from the others by quite a bit. No point exploring further, I'd just stash the juice behind one of the curtains and—

"Don't know where to put them, right?"

I jumped. For real this time. Bottles scattered, and my screech would have done a *bean sídhe* proud. My hands flew to my chest, and I wheezed in a breath. "Holy shit, you scared me. Good thing those are plastic bottles or I'd have a real mess on my hands." I looked down. His feet were bare. Anger flashed, heightened by the adrenaline pouring through me. "You meant to scare me, to catch me doing something—"

"Illegal." Porter's smile eased some of the threat in his voice.

I hadn't found a good opportunity to scan him, but his accusation could turn into a blatant threat, so to protect myself I'd have to do it right now. I skimmed the edge of my inside-out energy, and opened my senses. Jace was surrounded by a predominately silver aura, and that meant he was a gifted intuitive, possibly psychic, as well as smart and adaptable. And then his energy flashed. A streak of pink. More than one. The delicate strands threaded with the silver, which made it look like they flickered on and off. So, a family guy. Romantic and loyal.

My heart fluttered. No wonder I was attracted to him.

"Caitlin?"

What had he asked? Illegal. "No, not illegal, Jace. Helpful." There was no hope for it but complete honesty. I backed against the wall, bracing myself. "Hannah didn't murder Thatcher, and neither did I. I've been in the Islands less than forty-eight hours, so don't have any credibility in the neighborhood. Hannah apparently has some history with the victim. That puts both of us solidly on your suspect list."

His stare bored into me. "I did a background check. You were questioned by the Metropolitan Police in relation to the death of Fion Connor."

Nausea slammed me. "My mother died from heart failure, Officer Porter." I squeezed my lips closed to keep from saying another word. Something about Jace Porter was off, and I wanted to know what. The coppers at home used silence to make suspects talk, so why not turn the tables?

It didn't take long before he nodded. "It was noted in the report." He paused. "Ted Thatcher was stabbed to death outside the Ola Boutique storage area. That takes care of the what, where, and the basics of how. What's your best guess on who did it?"

Exhaustion seeped into my bones. "I have no idea." It was a heartfelt statement. "More than anything, I wish I knew, and could lead you right to him."

"Him?" The question drifted from Porter's mouth, almost as an afterthought. And there was no doubt he meant to trip me up.

I shuddered. "A guess. Doesn't it take a lot of strength to stab someone? Besides being a violent way to kill." I shrugged. "In the mysteries I read, women usually go for poison." Or magic. But I kept that to myself.

Jace dropped his flip-flops on the floor, and then inched his toes around the thong. Crazy, but somehow it was sexy. Jace had...elegant feet. "Women are capable of heinous acts, Caitlin."

He'd get no argument from me there. I decided to come clean, and held my hands out, fingers spread. "Look, I don't have a clue who stabbed Thatcher. That's why I'm here. I ran into Hannah's former fiancé, and he mentioned they broke it off because of her witchcraft. It seems Thatcher had been stalking her, trying to get her to create a curse for him."

Porter's eyes turned a lighter shade of brown, almost green. "Fits." He wandered toward a locked display case that was tucked into in corner nook.

I hadn't noticed it before, but now it was sending my internal magic into spastic overdrive. I stepped over the juice bottles, homing in on the display. It was odd, like some kind of compulsion I couldn't stop or deny. And, yeah, it scared the shitiski out of me. "Those are witchcraft tools. We all have a pentacle, wand, chalice, and athame. Often several of each. And we obviously use Tarot cards, candles, and herbs."

"Athame?" Porter asked.

"Yes, as you can see, they're double-edged daggers. They most often represent the element of fire, and we use them for ritual purposes like casting a circle, to cut or reseal a door in a circle, to charge or consecrate objects, and banish negative energy." Talking about it made me want to touch mine, just for reassurance. I'd only used it for clearing the negative energy from Fion's estate, but maybe one day I'd have the strength to call my energy and cast a circle. No. That was a terrible idea. A Gypsy witch had to be my highest calling.

Porter nodded, and shoved his hands in his pockets. "It could also be a weapon, and Matthews acknowledges her ties to the Craft. Always has."

I tensed, horrified at the idea. "Hannah would never use her athame to harm someone! No good witch would *ever* do such a thing, and she's good. You know she is. Her aura is golden."

Silence stretched.

Certainty spread through me. "You know her. Before this, you were friends."

He drew in a long breath. "Yes. Like you said, she was engaged to a fellow officer, and I agree she's a good person."

Spinning around, I pointed toward the bulletin board. "That's them."

He followed my gaze, forehead creased. "It is."

Now we were getting somewhere. "Yamoto Nori."

"Yes. You didn't say where you met him." Jace's stare drilled a hole through my plan to prevaricate.

Panic flared. I was well and truly caught, and since lying would dig me into a dreadful bit of a mess, I came clean. "Here. He was checking the premises when I came in to clean up."

Officer Porter took in the interior of Ola's with a slow inspection. "Shot protocol to hell. Why was he here?"

I lifted my shoulders, dropped them. "How would I know?"

Jace Porter's grin sent shivers into the pit of my stomach. Good ones. "You, Caitlin Connor, can't lie worth a damn."

Bloody hell. "I'm really *not* sure, but I think he still loves Hannah, and maybe did a stupid thing because he wants to help her. He seemed like a good sort, you know?"

"Yeah, I know." His sigh drifted through the shop. "He wanted to settle down and have a family, but the witchcraft threw him."

There was something... "But you're okay with witchcraft?"

"Oh, yes, Caitlin. I am."

Chapter 8

THE MOON (REVERSED)

*Hidden truths emerge
from the depths.*

THE INTERIOR OF OLA BOUTIQUE CLOSED IN ON ME, and I inhaled small puffs of spicy, incense-laced oxygen. Jace Porter *liked* me in a male-female sort of way. It was information overload, and the timing couldn't have been worse.

Still, a corner of my mouth quirked up in an uncontrollable smile, because I liked him, too. A lot. Or maybe I was infatuated with those ever-changing eyes. "Are you a witch?" I figured there was no harm in asking.

"Not me. My father is clairvoyant, sees future events, but not often, and only when something critical hangs in the balance." He'd relaxed some, and his cop persona had shifted to the background, making the real Jace easier to see.

My hands were resting on the top of the glass display case, and the Tarot decks were practically vibrating with an urgent message I couldn't ignore. So I scooted around Jace, hustling toward the boutique's front door where I'd dropped my handbag at Officer Nori's armed demand. But before I acted on the urgency vibrating from the cards, I needed to set the stage with Jace. "So, okay. We're here, and neither of us is breaking any laws. The boutique door was unlocked, I stepped in to tidy up for Hannah, you saw me through the window, and stopped to say hello. End of story, right?"

"More or less. What are you doing?" His eyes flashed a deep shade of green. I pegged it for curiosity.

I scooped my bag off the floor, and pulled out my Tarot deck. "I need to do a spread. Right now. My intuition has been screaming at me for a couple hours, but between Officer Nori and you, there's been no time." I stepped behind the checkout counter, shoved a business card holder and decorative pen container to one side, and breathed, slow and deep.

To his credit, Jace didn't so much as twitch.

But I did. Rain burst from the heavy cloud layer that had been hanging around since just before lunch. It drummed on the boutique roof with a deafening roar. I tipped my head back, warily scanning the ceiling. "I hope it doesn't leak."

Jace smiled. "And now you understand why they tented the crime scene. Rain is a constant in island life."

"I've never heard a simple downpour make its presence known quite so loudly." Turning back to the task at hand, I took a minute or two to quiet my frazzled nerves, to ground myself, then I blessed the countertop, and glanced up. "I'm going to do a reading for clues about who killed Thatcher."

Jace leaned forward. "Can I watch?" Genuine interest hummed in his tone.

A tiny voice in the corner of my heart mumbled, *be careful*, but there wasn't a convenient reason to say no, so I squashed my reluctance. "Sure."

He moved closer. "Will you talk me through it?"

Warm vibrations tickled my skin. Not only was Jace accepting my witchcraft, but he was seriously acknowledging the cards had a story to reveal. "I usually only talk when I'm reading for a client, but yes. I don't have anything to hide." I took in a calming breath, shuffled the cards, cut the deck, and prepared to begin my layout. "I'm doing a horseshoe spread, and before you ask, it wasn't a conscious choice. More like a compulsion. The cards tell me how they want to be arranged." I glanced at him sideways, and noted a calm expression with no sign of this-is-one-crazy-witch tightening his eyes or lips.

I tapped my finger on the top card in the deck. "This will be the significator. I'm asking that it represent the murderer." I laid the card down, turning it face up. The breath heated in my lungs. I gulped. The reversed Queen of Swords stared up at me. "This is the killer queen. She's cold, ruthless, vindictive, and unable to control her anger."

A low grumble sounded from across the counter, and I looked at Jace. "Do you think whoever offed Thatcher is a woman? Or maybe a man with Queen of Swords characteristics?"

His gaze held mine. "Doesn't matter what I think. We need to treat this intel like any other evidence, no preconceived theories. Just the facts. Theories follow facts in a solid investigation."

"Okay. A ruthless, vindictive person. The next card symbolizes past conditions." I laid down the Five of Cups, and considered what to say. "Cups are emotion, love, things like that. The five indicates disappointment, grieving, and depression. But this was in the past, so I'm guessing whatever is behind Thatcher's murder began as a male-female relationship gone arseways."

Jace scoffed. "Nothing surprising there."

I nodded agreement, then moved to the next card. "This one will be her present situation." I held my breath, hoping for a definitive clue. "Reversed Ten of Cups. That would be the end of happiness, probably referring to the romance. I wonder how long it lasted." I selected another card, requesting clarity, and then laid it on top of the Ten of Cups. "Nine of Swords. Anguish. Backstabbing. It could be nine days, months, or years, but I'm not getting a strong gut feeling for any of them."

"Probably not days if it led her to homicide," Jace said. "At least I hope it took the killer longer than a week to build up so much hate."

He got that right. Dusk was coming up fast, and it probably wasn't in our best interest to turn on any lights. I laid down the next card, in a hurry to finish the spread before it got too dark to see the cards. "The reversed Six of Cups is in the future position. Lots of passion in this spread, but then I guess violent crime is passionate by definition."

"No shit." Jace tapped the card. "What does it mean?"

"Stuck in the past. Longing for days gone by. Maybe

she...or he...lost Thatcher and wanted him back. Was he ever married?"

"Ongoing investigation, so I can't say much except I'll look into it."

The sanctity of police investigations was common knowledge. I respected it, but there was no harm in prodding him a bit. "Thatcher is dead, so I'm surprised the future is showing his killer longing for the past." I wanted more clarity, but in the interest of time drew the next card. "Next up is the best approach to the situation." I turned over the reversed Six of Wands. "Retreat from battle. Plans go sideways." I shook my head. "I'm guessing whoever murdered him isn't going to confess, no matter what this card says.

Jace made a keep going gesture.

"Attributes of others surrounding the killer. This one should be interesting." I shivered. Interesting maybe, but not in a good way. I turned over the High Priestess. It slipped from my fingers and landed crossways, not upright, not reversed. I stifled a tiny gasp. "Hannah."

"What?" Jace grabbed my hand. "Why'd it turn that way?"

"I don't know. It just slipped. Upright it signifies intuition, hidden knowledge, and keeping secrets. Reversed it means you've lost touch with your inner voice." I waited a beat. "I think it represents Hannah, Jace." His name tasted right on my tongue, and it bathed my insides with a sweet, warm glow.

"Not surprising. Most persons of interest keep secrets, especially in homicide cases. It's human nature. Detective

Stone will probably finish questioning her tonight."

Hope rippled through me. "You believe she's innocent, then."

He sidestepped the comment. "If he arrests her, she'll make bail soon. Keep going, hmm?"

I wanted to toss the deck of cards at him, but drew the next one instead, placed it down, and smiled. "This one represents challenges to be faced. The reversed Queen of Cups is moody, hysterical, pretty much a bitch. Fits a murderess, don't you think?"

Jace smiled, slightly crooked. "Agreed."

"The final outcome," I said, laying down the Tower. "In a general sense, this one symbolizes startling, radical change. But it also can indicate violence and hostility." I stepped back from the counter, and surveyed the spread. "So, you're going to look into Thatcher's love life, and I'm going to—"

"Go surfing, sightsee, anything but stick your nose into this case. Got it?"

Lost in his ever-changing eyes, I nodded in complete and total false agreement. And kept nodding until the front door banged open.

There stood Hannah.

Chapter 9

THREE OF WANDS

Plan your next move.

STARKLY DEFINED AGAINST THE DARK SKY, HANNAH stood in the doorway of Ola Boutique, a whirlwind of energy surrounding her. It sent shivers into the pit of my stomach. The woman was one bloody powerful witch.

Jace blew out a labored breath with a whispered, "Shit," floating on his exhalation.

Hannah stepped through the doorway. "Time for you to leave, Officer. Now." Her glare bored into him, and my shivering stomach knotted into a hard ball of dread.

Jace shot me a sideways glance, then made tracks for the door. "On my way, Ms. Matthews." He closed the door so gently there wasn't a trace of sound. Guess he didn't want to take a chance on upsetting an already furious witch.

Hannah turned to lock the door, made sure the Closed sign faced out, and then sloughed rain from her arms.

Adrenaline spiked along with my panic. Locked in a

confined space with an angry witch. Not good. Like Jace, I didn't want to poke at her anger, so I started to gather my Tarot cards.

Her soft voice stilled my panic. "Don't touch the cards. Please. I'd like to see them. What were you divining?"

I faced her. Her aura was vibrating smoothly, the gold was strong and vibrant, and only a trace of angry red floated around the edges. Besides, I was also a witch, and powerful. Maybe my experience wasn't equal to hers yet, but I could hold my own if she attacked. "Who killed Thatcher."

Her posture, her bones eased. "You believe I'm innocent?" Hope threaded beneath her words.

Surely she didn't think... "Of course you didn't kill him. It would be all over your aura, and, aside from the silvery gray witch fog, your energy is golden and sparkly." I'd seen several post-death auras around the people who'd witnessed my parents' souls leaving their bodies. The colors faded to shadows, and the person's vibration slowed. Still...there *was* that gray fog around Hannah.

She closed the distance between us. "Your sight is strong, and I thank you for your support. Now, will you tell me about your spread?"

Her gratitude was palpable, and all trace of anger had dissipated. My inner witch pushed at me, wanting to make friends with Hannah's inner witch. No point fighting the inevitable, so I waved my hand over the cards. "Do you read at all?"

"Some, but I'm exhausted and would love to hear your take on the...incident." She eyed the bottles of juice still lying on the floor. "Wait. I could use a drink. You?"

I licked my lips. Dry. "Yes, thanks. Anything but pineapple. It's the only option in my refrigerator, and I've already had two big glasses in a short time. My stomach says enough."

Hannah grabbed two bottles of banana coconut juice, and handed me one. "This has a gentle flavor. Now, what about your spread?"

I tuned into my intuition, and went over every card exactly the way I had with Jace. Hannah silently drank her juice without commenting, and the silence battered at my confidence. I'd been reading less than a year, had barely accepted my witch DNA, so it was unnerving to voice my divination to a woman well-trained in the Craft.

When I finished, she rested her hand on my shoulder. "Nice work, Caitlin. I like the feel of your energy in the Ola space."

Courage straightened my spine. "Thanks. It's an easy place to do a reading, welcomes the energy. So, what can you add? Thatcher was a customer, so you must have an intuitive reaction to him."

She nodded, slid the stool out from behind the counter, and sat.

I sighed, fatigue spreading through my muscles.

Hannah laughed, hoarsely, like she hadn't done it for a while. "Grab a stool from one of the dressing rooms and join me."

I made it to the rear of the shop and back in record time, planted myself, and gave Hannah my full attention.

She held up her hand. "First, tell me what you learned

from Yamato. He left trails of energy all over everything, and I'll need to do a thorough clearing, but not before I've gathered every trace of information about his visit."

Damn, how had I missed that? There was still so much for me to learn about witchcraft. I blew out a frustrated sigh, and then shared everything I could remember from my conversation with Yamato, ending with how I'd practically shoved him out of the shop.

Hannah upended her juice, draining the bottle. "Thatcher wandered through the shop a few times a week, and left behind clinging tendrils of shattered pink energy. It was easy to clear, so I didn't worry about his apparent crush on me. But after Yamato and I were engaged, when he noticed my ring, violence spiked through his aura. I banned him from the shop, and he complied for a few weeks."

Empathic chills slithered along my spine. "Did you get a restraining order?"

"No. They don't do a lot of good, and I thought I'd handled it. He didn't show up again, but started sending me emails. At first they were requests for a curse, something simple to keep enemies at bay, but without violence. Of course I refused, explained my ironclad philosophy of doing no harm, and that I would never generate a curse, period."

I nodded. We were definitely kindred spirits philosophy-wise. My heart warmed, and my apprehension about Hannah evaporated with one beautiful swoosh of energy. Sometimes I appreciated the blessing of being a witch, because things like trust were quickly corroborated with an aura scan. It's the only reason I decided to use any of my inside-out energy. The good outweighed the bad...as long as I could control how much of it I accessed.

Hannah held my gaze. "And then he broke into Ola. Of course, I recognized his energy imprint immediately."

I followed her train of thought. "But there was no way to explain it to the coppers."

"Exactly. Yamato believed me, was able to trace the crime to Thatcher, but the rat bastard disappeared before an arrest could be made...until today." She slumped wearily, her voice dragging.

I squeezed her hand. "We'll deal with this. My cousin, Everly, and her husband will help when they get back. They understand magic."

Hannah eased her hand from under mine. "Thanks. Detective Stone hasn't arrested me, but I'm their primary suspect." She rolled her lips in tight. "I'm scared, Cait."

"Yeah. Me, too, but we're in this together, and we're strong witches with honed intuition." I'd exaggerated—about myself anyway—but my emotional support seemed to smooth the worry from her eyes.

Hannah circled her head, stretching her neck muscles, and then tapped the Queen of Swords. "There's more. Yamato investigated Thatcher, learned he was married, then divorced. He didn't find copies of the paperwork, but your spread shows it was an acrimonious parting."

Some of my tension released. "So she's probably Thatcher's killer, right?"

With a headshake, Hannah destroyed my slim glimmer of hope. "She lives on the mainland, and Thatcher gave me the distinct impression she never leaves home."

Silence spread between us, and Hannah's attention seemed to have drifted. She was completely focused on the area at the rear of the shop. And then she faced me with a huge smile that made her face glow.

Chapter 10

JUDGMENT

*You are being called
to something greater.*

LINES HAD BEEN ETCHED IN HANNAH'S FACE WHEN SHE arrived at the boutique, but her smile had erased them completely, leaving her skin luminous. "Your readings are excellent, and you said this was your first day on Island."

I nodded, at a loss as to what she was thinking, or why she was suddenly so happy.

"Have you done any retail work?" she asked.

What the heck? But I didn't see any harm in answering. "Not really. I worked as a server in a pub, and also in a tearoom. And I've been running my mother's estate for the last nine months. The only connection to retail work would be a familiarity with accounting and using a point of sale system."

Her smile faded to a grimace. "I suspect I'm going to be tied up for some time, either with finding whoever murdered Thatcher, or held in jail until Detective Stone figures it out. I'd prefer the former, but... What do you think about a trial partnership of sorts? We could work on establishing my innocence, and share the shop responsibilities."

She must have sensed my doubt. "I know it's sudden to suggest something so significant, but we're witches, and we've been able to read each other in ways most people can't. I'm a little desperate here, Cait."

It wasn't what I wanted to do. Well, I did want to chase down the killer, because of my new calling to truth and justice, but retail work didn't fit at all. "I'm not the shop girl type. Honestly, I'm on the lookout for a place to do my Tarot readings."

Hannah leapt up. "Ola is the perfect place. Follow me."

She'd possibly slipped a cog. Who wouldn't, with the day she'd endured, so I followed her—just in case intervention was needed.

Hannah hurried toward the back of the shop, stopped in front of the curtained area at the very end of the hallway, and whipped the fabric back. "Look at this, Cait. It would be perfect for readings. It's out of the way, far enough from the dressing rooms to be private, and there's enough space for a nice-sized table and two comfortable chairs. What do you think?"

My brain cells spun with hope, and excitement. Gingerly I peeked into the cubicle, and the rightness of it slammed into me. "It's bloomin' perfect."

Hannah touched my shoulder. We were about to become partners. Panic mingled with a sense of how ideal this was. It was the right thing. No doubt there, but I wasn't good at sharing. And we'd be collaborating on a murder as well as a business.

I used my witchy senses to examine the room. It shimmered with light, and something...evil. "What is *that*?"

Hannah closed her eyes and drew in a long breath. And then she turned so pale, her face turned faintly blue. "It's death, Caitlin."

Stepping into the cubicle, she hunkered down, and lifted a stack of cloths. "What the fuck?"

I leaned forward, peering over her shoulder.

A bloody athame rested at Hannah's fingertips.

She swung to face me, wide, scared eyes boring into me. "It's mine. My athame, but I didn't kill him, Cait. I swear I didn't."

I slid farther into my darkness than I usually do, because a deep read on Hannah's aura was critical to any decisions I made from this point on. I closed my eyes to see more clearly.

She waited, her breathing ragged.

Clear and still gold at the core. Fear clouded the surface, but I would have been worried if it didn't. I breathed out a long sigh of relief. There was no sign of violence. Absolutely none. I opened my eyes and bent to touch her shoulder. "I had to look."

She nodded. "I would have done the same. What am I going to do, Cait?"

I stared at the bloody athame. Tremors started in my knees and worked their way up until I was too unsteady to stand. I sank to the floor next to Hannah. "Don't touch it."

She shrugged, defeated. "It already has my prints all

over it. I use it every day. At least I did until recently. It's been missing, and I thought one of my customers picked it up by mistake." She let out a soft grunt. "I guess maybe they did, only not by mistake. Someone is trying to frame me. The question is, who would do such a thing?"

"We should start working on that right away." There was no way for this to fly under our good detective's radar. "And, you realize we need to call Stone and hand it over."

Hannah braced her hand on my shoulder, and then stood. "Yes. I'll call right now."

I followed her, both of us backing out of the cubicle. "Ola's will be closed until the police finish gathering evidence from the back room, but after they leave we need to do a thorough clearing of the store."

"No shit," I said. It was a huge understatement. "There should be traces of the evil energy all through the shop, especially if it came from one of your customers. They'd have to leave trails of energy from the front door to the back hallway, wouldn't they?"

Hannah, frowned. "Yes. And I didn't feel it. Did you?"

I shook my head.

With a final wary glance toward the rear of the shop, Hannah picked up the phone and started punching numbers.

TEN TENSE MINUTES LATER, DETECTIVE Stone strolled into Ola Boutique, wearing jeans, a t-shirt, and a scowl that said he'd been off duty. He nodded a brief hello in our direction. "Back room?" He pointed in the correct direction.

"Yes, sir." Hannah said, her voice trembling. "I'll show you."

He held up his hand. "No. Wait here." After slipping paper booties over his shoes, he headed toward the cubicle.

A police SUV parked in front of the shop, and before Stone wound his way through the display racks and cases, two CSI technicians rapped on the door and entered.

"That way," Hannah said, pointing.

Weak and worried, I plopped onto one of stools behind the counter, and dropped my head into my hands. This was such a bloody mess.

"I'm innocent, Cait. This will all work itself out, but I'm afraid it's one of those situations that's going to get worse before it gets better." The tension in her voice sent fear licking down my spine, so I did another quick scan of her aura. Yep, there was some shredding in her energy field. And she was clearly hiding something.

I peered at her through my fingers. "It's bad, and there's something you're not telling me."

She sat on the other stool, and ignored my prod for more information. "How about we use this time for some training?"

What the hell? Now? With police and crime scene techs crawling all over the place? My expression must have broadcasted my thoughts, because Hannah tapped the iPad attached to a small stand. "Might be my only opportunity to show you how to use this new-fangled point of sale system."

Her witchy senses were definitely more honed than mine, but I expected she was right. I blew out a breath in an attempt to clear my mind. "Okay. Let's do it."

She showed me the cash drawer, and then removed a thin notebook from the top shelf behind the counter. She held it up, then handed it to me. "All the information you'll need to run Ola's is in here, so you have backup in case you don't remember what I'm going to show you."

Some of the pressure released from my chest. Backup information was good.

We were almost finished with her crash course in retail management when Detective Stone strode toward us. "Hannah Matthews, you're under arrest for the murder of Theodore Thatcher."

I jumped to my feet. "You can't be serious."

His glare shut me up. I turned to Hannah. "I'll contact your attorney, and we'll have you out early tomorrow morning."

She closed her eyes, breathed out two deep sighs, then stared into Stone's eyes. "The phone call I heard come in while you were in the back just now. They told you the swabs you took from my hands were positive for Thatcher's blood type, didn't they?" Her words held desperation and defeat.

I gasped, then snapped my mouth shut. How in the bloody hell had Hannah gotten Thatcher's blood on her hands?

She must have read my expression, because she gave me a twisted smile. "It's all right, Caitlin." She turned to Stone. "If you could have one of your officers get the keys from my purse, and give them to Caitlin, we can be on our way." Her smile was sharp-edged. "You'd rather me not go digging in my bag, right?"

Stone's nod was brisk. "Turn around, hands behind your back."

Hannah complied, and it shattered my heart when the handcuffs clicked into place. She didn't so much as lay a finger on Thatcher, much less end his life. I'd been instrumental in my mother's death, and yet Hannah was the one going to prison. It was just plain wrong.

It was Officer Fields who searched for Hannah's keys, then handed them to me, and escorted her to the waiting patrol car.

Irritation and guilt morphed into solid anger, and I turned on Stone. "How could you? She's innocent, and you know it."

"Evidence and orders." His tone was clipped. "The techs have finished here, so I'm not going to close the shop." He shook his head. "Officer Porter informed me about your Tarot reading. I need facts to back it up, Caitlin." And with that he spun on his heel and left.

The crime scene techs had left just before Stone arrested Hannah, which left only Officer Fields and me. The sudden quiet weighed heavy on my nerves.

"If you'd like to lock up, Ms. Connor, Detective Stone requested I give you a ride home."

No way *that* was going to happen. I'd shared all the face time with law enforcement I could stomach. "Please go on home, or whatever. I live down the road, and I'd rather walk. It'll help clear my head after all...this."

His forehead knotted. "Orders. I have to see you safely home."

Heat blasted through me, and I would have sworn my hair crackled with magic. "To get me in your patrol car, Officer, you're going to have to arrest me. Is that clear enough?"

He backed up a step, showing me how right I was about the crackling energy. There are times when magic was my best friend, I only hoped my temper hadn't tapped into the darkness. Sometimes I couldn't tell.

Fields's gulp was audible. "I'll just call your request in and be on my way. You watch yourself."

I tossed Hannah's keys in the air, caught them. I would have attempted a conciliatory smile, but in my present mood, it probably would have scared the shitiski out of him. "You can count on it."

After he left, I locked the door behind him and took a walk through the shop. I needed to assess the evil energy in the back room one more time, do a simple energy clearing to hold things together until tomorrow morning, when I'd be rested and up to doing a full circle cleansing of the shop. A full circle. It would be my first one, and would necessitate using more inside-out energy than I was comfortable with. But I had no choice. Dawn would be the best time.

Evil still clung to the back room, but it was contained. My mind eased a bit. I checked the case where Hannah displayed the Wiccan tools, and sighed with relief when I spotted everything else I'd need for the morning ritual. I'd have to go over the process a few times to be sure I got it right. There was a lot to learn about embracing witchcraft, and my grimoire was safely resting on my dresser at home.

I never thought I'd have to use it. Strange how life changes.

I left a softly lit lamp burning on the checkout counter, strolled out of the shop, and carefully locked the door behind me.

I'd only made it four or five steps before a man stepped in front of me, blocking my path. My shriek lost momentum when I recognized Jace's scent. The man smelled like wind-kissed ocean, and I savored a second, deeper inhalation. "You scared me, Jace. For the third time today."

"Didn't mean to. I've been watching from OTB. Wanted to make sure you were okay before I headed home."

There might have been some truth in what he said, but there was also a lot he didn't say. "I'll be fine. As fine as I can be with Hannah arrested." I shot him a sideways glance. "Did you know?"

"Not until I saw them take her away. I didn't think there was enough evidence to make an arrest yet," he said.

"Hannah mumbled something about Thatcher's blood showing up on her hands. How can that be possible? Oh, and Stone also said something about orders. And then he told me you gave him the particulars of my Tarot spread, and said he needed evidence to back it up. Guess I better get busy finding the real murderer."

He choked. "No. That is *not* what Detective Stone was suggesting—at all."

My inner "wicked" witch bubbled to the surface, and I batted my eyelashes at him. "Maybe. Maybe not, but I'll be using his lack of specificity as permission to do what I need to do. Witches stand by their own." I bloody well sound like Hannah, and it had me grinning. And then it hit me. "Oh, no. I want to be here at dawn to clear the shop, and I don't have a cell phone or any other way to wake up."

Jace tugged a mobile from his back pocket. "I have one, and I have early duty call tomorrow. How about I stop by your place and rap on the door until I see signs of life?"

I was not ready for Jace to see me with bed head and in total dishabille, but his suggestion was my only option. "That would be nice of you, and way beyond your protect and serve motto."

My expression must have bordered on terrified, because he winked. "I promise to stay outside and only knock until I hear your voice through the door. Does that work?"

It did, and relief spun through me. "Here." I reached for his phone. "I'll add my address to your contact list."

He tapped a few keys, then handed his mobile over. "Tomorrow we'll get you a new phone. It's not safe, especially under the circumstances, for you not to have communication at your fingertips."

My nerves kicked up a notch. "*We'll* get me a new phone?" I asked, passing his mobile back after I typed in my address.

Jace's eyebrows lifted for a second. "Did I overstep? Sorry. I have a friend at the Verizon store, and I know he'll be able to give you a good deal. Thought it might be helpful."

Damn, but I hated to be caught acting the wanker. "No, I'm sorry. There's just been so much going on..."

A breeze gusted around us, blowing my hair across my face. Jace caught the loose strands, and tucked them behind my ear. "It feels like black silk. Pretty. I'll walk you home, Cait."

A warm bubbly feeling exploded in my chest. It was a bit scary. "My hair isn't actually black. More like mahogany with red highlights."

"I'll be sure and do a thorough examination in the sunlight." His grin was full of teasing promise.

Happy fear twisted me all up. "You don't have to..."

The protest died on my lips when he slipped his hand around mine, and threaded our fingers together. For the first time since tripping over Thatcher's shoe, I was positive I had the strength to live my destiny. To stand for truth and justice.

An it harm none.

The Chariot

Caitlin's Tarot: Episode 2

It was going to be a witchy kind of day...

Working at the Ola Boutique wasn't in Caitlin's plans, but it provides the perfect opportunity to build a following for her Tarot readings, and to search for whoever killed Ted Thatcher. Her destiny, standing for truth and justice, demands she find the murderer, and free Ola Boutique's owner, Hannah Matthews, from being convicted of a crime she didn't commit.

New to working with her Wiccan heritage, Caitlin casts her first circle with unexpected and disturbing results that lead her into uncharted territory.

How will Caitlin find the guilty witch when she's barely dipped her toes into the Craft? And what if the guilty witch really is Hannah?

Chapter 1

THREE OF WANDS

Investigating new directions.

IT WAS GOING TO BE A WITCHY KIND OF DAY. AND that meant I had to step out of my comfort zone and do a full body immersion into pure white energy. Panic surged through me, a perfect contrast to my mutant DNA.

I'd fallen asleep over my grimoire, cheek pressed to the pages, and nose tucked against the binding. Not at all cozy, but even after two pots of coffee my body sort of gave out, until I jerked awake when Officer Jace Porter rapped on my condo door at precisely four thirty in the morning, just as he'd promised. I cracked the blinds open to wave him off and assure him I was up and moving, but waited until he was safely in his patrol car before I opened the door to catch a glimpse of dawn radiating low on the horizon. The threat of night passing too quickly into morning pushed me to intensify my search for instructions on how to cast a circle.

Hours of reading the faded, cramped handwriting of bygone witches left me sure of only one thing. The best time to cleanse the energy in Ola Boutique was daybreak, but I'd yet to find any step-by-step instructions.

It didn't help that I was a cranky morning person. I gulped the dregs of my umpteenth cup of coffee, and shuddered when it hit my taste buds. Cold. Bitter. Nasty. It mimicked my mood perfectly. Tripping over Ted Thatcher's murdered body yesterday had not only pissed me off, but brought out a rare and uncomfortable streak of bitchiness. Hawaii was supposed to have been my idyllic new home. But no, it turned out to be my destiny instead.

In the whirlwind of events following my discovery of Thatcher, I'd ended up business partners with Hannah Matthews, witch extraordinaire. And that meant I needed to clear "our" shop of all negative energy before ten o'clock. My witching hour, so to speak.

Fortunately the boutique was only a fifteen-minute walk from my condo, so I wasn't completely out of time. Yet. Determined, I turned back to the ancient grimoire's fragile pages and thumbed through dozens of complex spells, but found nothing helpful. A fresh blast of panic knotted my insides. Maybe casting was innate for witches, a simple task most were able to do in their sleep—and certainly by the time they were out of primary school. Ordinary witches probably didn't need circle-casting instructions.

Pisser. I slammed the grimoire shut. What would Hannah do? Or my cousin, Everly? Both of them were psychically gifted, and well versed in the paranormal. I bounced up from the sofa and paced for a minute or two, then grabbed the blessed book and marched outside.

The power of the ocean swirled around me, and by the goddesses I was going to use it. I placed the grimoire in the center of my patio table, closed my eyes, and let the sound of the waves crash over me.

I'd never tried to tap into energy other than what I'd been born with, but I was desperate for help. After several deep breaths I relaxed into the ancient rhythm, and then opened the grimoire, blindly selected a page, and finally opened my eyes and read: *Casting a Clearing Circle.*

It was that simple; and that frustrating. Apparently all I had to do was ask the bloody book to show me what I needed to know.

THIRTY MINUTES LATER I UNLOCKED Ola Boutique, stepped inside, and then double-checked that the door was firmly locked behind me. I didn't want any interruptions. Unloading my duffle on the counter, I headed for the rear of the shop, where Hannah displayed Ola's assortment of Wiccan supplies. According to my grimoire, casting needed to be done in a space that had been physically cleaned and purified with a witch hazel solution, and I was positive I'd seen several bottles lined up on one of the display shelves.

Yes, on the far right top shelf. I blew out a sigh of relief, stretched on tiptoes to grab one, mixed it one-part-to-ten with water, and set about scrubbing all the wooden floors and countertops. From my late-night research, I'd learned this step was a critical prelude to casting a circle when there was negative energy in the space. And Ola Boutique was chock full of negative energy, including leftover auric trails from Ted Thatcher, a bunch of coppers, and the murder weapon.

Following the directions from my grimoire, I worked in a counterclockwise direction—widdershins, in witchy terminology—to banish the negativity. First I scrubbed the floors, then the countertops. All very mundane, which made it easy to get into the rhythm, but it still took far longer than I expected.

I placed my grimoire, athame, Tarot cards, candles and lighter in the space I'd chosen for the circle, then stepped to the center, and sucked in a preparatory breath. I was ready, except for one tiny detail.

Witches cast circles for protection because metaphysical energy attracts spiritual beings, or so my research into witchcraft said. Who knew? And it really sucked, because Ted Thatcher's soul had returned to the ethereal fold in the alley behind Ola's. What if it was still hanging around, waiting for his murderer to be brought to justice? The thought had my arm hairs standing on end, so I planted my hands on my hips, and glared at the ceiling. "Just so everyone is clear about this, I'm casting this circle to *clear* all negative energy, including any attached to Ted Thatcher." That should do it. Oh, wait. I quickly added an addendum. "Or any other persons or beings."

Satisfied, I double-checked the instructions in my grimoire. Four steps. I could do this. I placed the candles in their appropriate locations— air, yellow, east; fire, red, south; water, blue, west; and earth, green, north. Next, I unwrapped my Tarot deck from the protective velvet cloth, and selected the four aces. After placing them in front of the candles—swords at the east, wands at the south, cups at the west, and pentacles at the north, everything was ready.

Just to be absolutely sure, I stood at the center of the circle, and slowly turned, making sure everything was in place. Nodding, I took a firm grip on my athame, pointed the tip down, envisioned a stream of white light flowing from it, and then walked the perimeter of my circle clockwise—deosil—three times.

Exchanging my athame for the candle lighter, I started in the east, and lit each candle, again clockwise, while I called on the guardian of that element to clear Ola Boutique of all negative energy, and to bless it as a safe place for me to do my Tarot readings.

I shivered. No backing out now. I sat in the center of the sacred space, closed my eyes, and imagined white light infusing the entire back of the shop with protective energy. Warmth cascaded over me from head to toe, and my eyes popped open. Seriously? The boutique was actually glowing with gorgeous white light. I thanked my witch genes I was able to see energy, because it was so very calming. Not at all scary like I thought it would be—considering it was the exact opposite of my dense energy. Which *was* damn scary.

It humbled me, a newbie witch, to be able to see the difference in energy. When it streamed from my athame, it was sharp and directed, so different from the diffuse, soft white light filling my circle from above. Tears filled my eyes, and I simply sat there, basking in the honor that had been bestowed on me, the energy thumping in my chest like a giant heartbeat.

Until a whirlwind of energy surrounded me, stealing my breath.

A rush of adrenaline hit me, and I fought to hold my ground.

A pale outline of Thatcher's body was in the circle *with* me. His *visible* body. Hovering over me.

"Bloody hell!" I jumped up, ready for battle. Thatcher's image was fuzzy, but when I squinted, I could see that his facial features looked identical to Jace Porter's drawing. No stab wounds. No blood. So ethereal bodies were able to ditch their worldly scars. What else could the spirits of dead people do?

I stomped on my panic. Other than the shock factor, there was no threat oozing from his...likeness. "What in the bloody hell are you doing in my circle?" I asked, my voice a few decibels louder than normal

Attitude poured from him, as if he owned the place. How could this be happening? Damn, but I was a daft cow. I'd set the intention to clear negative energy. It would have been okay if I hadn't added *including* Ted Thatcher's. And, double crap, I'd added that bit about all other persons and beings.

Frantic, I spun around, checking out every inch of my circle. No other bodies floated in the background. Either there weren't any ghosts hanging around the shopping mall, or none of them held negative energy. Thank the goddesses for that. But Thatcher did, or he wouldn't be here.

I faced the apparition. "Who killed you?" No point

wasting a perfectly good opportunity to chat up the dead body in question.

Witch. The single word settled in my brain with hollow tenacity, leaving me a wobbly-kneed mess. "No. That can't be."

The whirlwind picked up speed.

Witch. It slammed me with the force of an angry shout, and then Ted Thatcher's ethereal body dissolved.

Chapter 2

TWO OF SWORDS

Armed peace. Uncertainty.

HANNAH! SHAKING, I DROPPED TO THE FLOOR. THE only witch connected with Thatcher was Hannah. I shook my head. Besides me, but I didn't kill him. She wasn't guilty, either. At least my gut didn't think so.

The energy bathing my circle was still vibrant, so I tried to quiet my mind and use it to make sense of what just happened. Pisser. I'd set an intention, cast my first circle, and bloody hell broke loose.

It was more than my brain could handle. The white light pulsing around me had spread to fill the inside of Ola's, and to my witch's eye the shop aura appeared to be clear and squeaky clean. There was nothing more for the circle to do. It had bloody well conjured Thatcher and his accusation, and that was more than enough.

Fingers trembling, I picked up my grimoire, and scanned down the page to the closing instructions. The words blurred, and tears streaked down my cheeks. The clean, positive energy was so strong, it had zapped me, mind and body. Raw emotion poured through me. I had summoned this pure white light. To have inadvertently conjured a dead man was incomprehensible. Especially since my inborn energy was dense as night. A faint glimmer of understanding about the power of witchcraft blossomed in my mind and heart. Humility was essential to the practice. The art was a gift, a blessing, and not to be taken lightly.

I swiped at my tears and focused on the grimoire. There was only one sentence. *Give thanks and reverse the order.*

I offered thanks to the white light, and, fighting for control of my muscles, stood. Starting in the north, I blew out each candle while thanking the guardians of its direction and element. I collected the candles and my Tarot cards, and finally walked the circle with my athame in a widdershins direction three times.

It was done.

The air in the boutique was light and clean, and there was no trace of Thatcher's energy, not even in the small back room where Hannah and I had found the murder weapon.

Her athame. Covered in Thatcher's blood. I shivered. The dead man's ethereal accusation left me no choice but to dig deeper into Hannah's role in the homicide. If working with white energy brought about this kind of shambles, in the future I'd stick with my inside-out DNA. At least it was predictably scary.

Because of Thatcher's unscheduled appearance, the clearing circle took more time than I expected, and now

I'd have to rush home to shower and dress, or I'd be late opening Ola Boutique for business. But there was one more thing I had to do first. Using my athame, I sketched a pentacle over the boutique door to protect Ola's from negative energy, and then I wrapped my dagger in a protective cloth and dropped it into my duffle, slung the bag over my shoulder, and shoved the door open.

The squeaky tight schedule was my only excuse for barreling into the man standing outside the entrance to Ola's.

THE END OF MY DUFFLE rammed Detective Stone smack in that tender spot just beneath his rib cage. He paled, then oofed out a grunt.

Bloody hell, I was already late, and now I'd inadvertently beat up on the one person who seemed honest enough to give Hannah a fair shake. "What a shambles. I'm sorry, Detective, I didn't spot you before I opened the door." Thank the holy heavens I hadn't hit him in the balls, or he'd see to it Hannah was locked up on death row for sure. Probably me too.

The blow must have knocked a kink in his diaphragm, because it took a minute before he straightened to his full, looking-down-on-me height. "Ms. Connor."

"Yes." I skimmed the edges of my dense energy, pulling at it just enough to see his aura. Green and strong, but there were some streaks of red threading along the edges. He was in a creative and practical mood, but the red was a sign of competitiveness. Still, the energy was calm, and no alarms were telling me to duck and cover.

Stone pointed at the end of my duffle.

I looked down. The tip of my athame was clearly outlined against the thin nylon fabric. Pisser. I shot a frantic glance at Stone's abdomen. No blood. "Are you hurt, then?"

His glare froze my bones. "I'm fine, but I'd like to see what rammed into me."

I could refuse, but that would be beyond stupid. "It's just my athame." I unzipped the end of the duffle, hauled out the dagger, and opened the protective cloth. I didn't offer it to him because I didn't want his energy to mingle with the beautiful white aura still clinging to it.

His stare pinned me in place. "Almost identical to the murder weapon."

Confused, I wrinkled my nose. "Not at all. Mine is shorter, slightly wider, and see?" I turned it over. "There's a pentagram at the base of the hilt. They're very different. Every witch is drawn to her own unique athame."

Detective Stone's lips twitched. "Of course. Entirely different, other than they're both daggers."

He had a point. I slipped the athame into my duffle, and then zipped it tight. Best to change the subject. "Were you here to see me? Has bail been set for Hannah?"

"No bail. I thought Officer Fields told you there was no chance this judge would set bail at Hannah's arraignment."

Tingles zipped along my nerves. Something was wonky. "*This* judge?"

Stone scrubbed his hand over his face. "He's golf buddies with my captain. They're both strongly convinced

Ms. Matthews is guilty, although she did plead not guilty. Another judge might have set bail, but even so it would be a minimum of one million, and require a nonrefundable hundred K down payment to a bail bondsman."

My stomach lurched. I didn't have that kind of money. Everly might, but she wasn't here, and even if she was, I couldn't ask, not when I had no way to repay her. "That's...a lot."

"Law enforcement and the courts take homicide seriously."

"But Hannah is innocent." For the first time, my voice lacked conviction.

Stone ignored my protest.

I tried another tactic. "When can I see her?"

"No visitors other than counselors, doctors, and lawyers. It's restricted in homicide cases."

A horrible sense of foreboding pounded in my chest. "But the shop. How will I manage if I can't go over the paperwork with her?" More importantly, how would I find the killer without Hannah's input?

Detective Stone scowled. "I'll request permission for you to have limited visitation, but I can't guarantee anything."

It would have to do. I gave him a glowing smile. "Thank you." And then I tossed in a smidgeon of helpless female. "I've never worked retail before. What if I make a total shambles of it?"

"Hmm, I expect you'll do fine." He tapped his watch. "Did you say you were running late?"

I caught a glimpse of the time, and hastily backed

away from Stone. "The cleaning, what with the bloody murder weapon being found inside..." I turned, breaking into a jog. "It took longer..." Damn, damn, damn. I had less than an hour to get back home, shower, find something suitable to wear, and make it back to Ola's to open by ten o'clock.

Or maybe it would be better to slap on any old clothes, and find something in the store to wear. Yes, that was a much better plan, and smart advertising as well. If only scrubbing the floor hadn't been such a dirty job, I could have showered first thing this morning, but I knew I'd have to wash the grime off after I cleaned. There was no help for it.

It was the fastest shower ever. And I could leave my hair down to dry while I walked back to the boutique, then I'd have to knot it semi-wet on top of my head. It was a conundrum. If I allowed it to dry naturally the curls would be unmanageable, but if I knotted it up soaking wet, it would stay soggy all day. Not a becoming look for me. Besides, I had to *walk* back to the shopping center. If I jogged, I'd be smelly and sweaty enough to scare away Hannah's customers.

There was a queue of people hanging about Starbucks, and I *needed* my chai. It would have to wait, though, because I just didn't have time to queue up in that line. I stepped over the threshold at Ola's, and closed the door behind me. Hannah had left it propped open yesterday, and I'd do the same, but not until I changed into an appropriate outfit.

I hadn't actually looked at any of the clothes she had

for sale, something I'd need to remedy right away, since I was now responsible for acting the role of proprietor. I was drawn to a rack of long dresses against the side wall, and sorted through them with a keen eye toward my new profession. I needed an outfit to fit my role as a Gypsy witch doing Tarot readings, but would also be fitting for a pseudo-owner of an upscale clothing boutique. In moments, I found the perfect dress—rich shade of purple, halter neckline, and the silk shimmered with mystery. I ducked behind the rack, stripped out of my shorts and t-shirt, and slipped the dress over my head. It swished, a most intoxicating sound, and the silk was cool against my skin. The maxi skirt was demure, but wild enough for the most discerning Gypsy. I loved it. Until I looked at the price tag. Over four hundred dollars with tax. Way out of my budget.

I reached to untie the halter top, but a woman rapped on the door, then pressed her nose to the glass. No time to change. Ola's should have been open ten minutes earlier. My heart tripped into double-time. My first customer, and I didn't have a clue about the merchandise Hannah carried. I scooped up my clothes, stuffed them behind the checkout counter, and opened the door, beaming a smile. "Welcome to Ola's. Please come in."

She scooted around me, trailing a heavy scent of lavender. "Thanks. You were supposed to open ages ago."

I hurried outside, gulped some fresh air, and scraped my foot on the sidewalk. Holy crap, I was barefoot. And the only shoes I had were cheap rubber flip-flops. Ah, slippahs. No matter what I called them, they wouldn't do as work shoes. My dress covered my feet, and the purple polish on my toes matched the fabric perfectly. If anyone commented, I might be able to get away with blaming my non-existent Gypsy heritage.

"Miss, I'm in a hurry here." There was enough bite in her tone to rival Detective Stone.

I hurried behind the counter, breathing through my mouth so I didn't dissolve into a sneezing fit. It didn't help much, since the woman's perfume tasted as bad as it smelled. It wasn't natural. Hannah had some essential oil candles displayed on the counter, and their fragrance was light and sweet. "I'll have you checked out straightaway."

She crumpled one of the super soft t-shirts, and stuck it under her arm while she dug for her credit card, then dropped them both on the counter.

I swiped her card, shook out the t-shirt, and started to fold it. She grabbed it from my hands. "It's too wrinkled. Get me another."

I'd been working retail for less than five minutes, and was mentally selecting an athame from the display case to stab this woman straight through the heart. But being new to the job, I gave her a toothy grin, noted the shirt size, then went to collect another one. "Here you are. All neat and tidy." I wrapped it in tissue, and bagged it before she could open her mouth with another complaint.

She headed for the door just as Officer Jace Porter strolled in.

Chapter 3

THREE OF CUPS

Friendship. Being understood and appreciated.

JACE HELD THE DOOR FOR MS. CRABBY CUSTOMER with his backside while balancing two Starbucks cups in his hands. "Morning, ma'am."

She stomped out, her elbow missing the cups by a millimeter.

He shot me a look, then shrugged before nudging the door closed with his foot. "What bit her?"

The wind-kissed ocean scent of him mixed with the coffee and chai. It swirled around me in a fascinating combination, and I drew in a breath to savor the texture of it. "I opened ten minutes late. Nasty bit of business for my first punter."

"Punter?" Jace's forehead wrinkled in that adorable confused expression he favored.

"Customer in Yank speak." I spread the offending t-shirt on the counter and smoothed out the wrinkles. "Quite the bitch. I was late opening, but still—"

He handed me the chai latte. "Did you go back to bed

after I woke you? I should've insisted you open the door and talk to me."

I took the cup, welcoming the warmth spreading through my palm. "Thanks for this. I was in desperate need. And no, I stayed up. Never made it to bed, actually. There were issues with the clearing ceremony this morning, and with it being my first and all, it took longer than I expected."

He must have heard the confusion beneath my words. "Issues, huh? Let me take a wild stab here. Wiccan issues are more complex than the ordinary, everyday variety?"

I took a swallow of chai, set it down, then pressed my lips together. I had to tell him enough to satisfy his curiosity, but the big question was how *little* could I get by with? "Yes. There's a lot of energy involved in casting."

I was twitchy from lack of sleep, too much caffeine, and my up close encounter with the dead, so I busied myself smoothing the wrinkles from the t-shirt.

Jace covered my hands with his. "How about you stop wearing a hole in that and talk to me? What exactly happened this morning?"

I sneaked a peek at his ever-changing eyes, wondering what color they'd surprise me with today. Gold. I stared, unable to look away from the warm shade that was a close match to Hannah's aura. After spending the morning with Thatcher's apparition, the coincidence was too much, and I blurted out my fear. "You're a copper."

Jace jerked his hand back. "I'm not here as cop, Caitlin."

I flicked my fingers at his chest. "Uniform. And you

were with Detective Stone yesterday."

He scrubbed his hand over his hair, leaving it little-boy tousled. "I'm an officer, yes. And I worked patrol when I first started, but not anymore. I'm a forensic artist who happens to have graduated from the police academy. Stone asked me to ride along yesterday because Fields gave him a heads-up the photographs would be too graphic for patrol officers to use when they canvassed the neighborhood."

He'd blurted out the words without pausing for breath, and it took me a minute to understand. "Does that mean you're not assigned to the case?"

"I wouldn't be here if I was. You must watch enough television to know it's against policy for an officer to be involved with anyone connected to one of their cases."

Something wild sparked and flashed in my chest. *Involved*? What did that mean, exactly? I nodded, mute, and busied myself folding the t-shirt.

Jace sighed, then lifted my chin with the tip of his index finger. "Other than scuttlebutt, I don't know shit about the details of *any* investigation, other than what directly pertains to the witness, and the crime I'm creating a sketch for. We *can* be friends."

I eased back from his touch, heat burning in my cheeks and spreading over my chest. He liked me. "Okay." The burn got hotter. I wasn't the sort to get tongue-tied.

"Nice dress," Jace said, his gaze slipping from my eyes down to my toes. "Bare feet. Is that a witch thing?"

"Oh, damn. I have to change. I mean, thank you. It is a nice dress, but it isn't mine. I thought it would be best to wear something from the shop, to advertise and all, but I still had to look the part of a Gypsy Tarot reader."

I slapped my hand over my mouth.

He shook his head. "You nailed it, so why not just buy the dress?"

I was suddenly aware of the price tag pressed snugly against my ribs. "There are four hundred reasons."

Jace's eyes narrowed for a minute, then opened wide. Green had mixed with the gold in the most delightful pattern. He turned the t-shirt tag over and gasped. "Eighty bucks for a t-shirt."

I smothered a grin. "Ola is an upscale boutique, and that's a Rag and Bone classic."

He blinked at me. "You wear these?"

He'd tossed it off like a casual question, but there was fear behind his eyes. "I own one. A hand-me-down from Everly. I borrowed it the day after..." I shrugged. "The particulars don't matter. She let me keep it, a personal thing to keep us connected."

"Uh-huh." Gingerly, he picked up the shirt, placed it atop the proper display, then strolled back to me. "Now, about the dress. Why don't you ask Hannah if you can have a clothing allowance while you're working here?"

I ran my palms down the luxurious silk covering my thighs. Tingles shimmered through my arms. "It's uncomfortable, like asking for a handout. Is that a normal thing in the States? For people working in retail?"

"My sister worked at Nordstrom for a while, and a store discount was one of her benefits. Now, how about we get back to you telling me what really happened this morning?"

Jace wasn't going to let this drop. And it would be so much easier if I could share with someone. I started to scan his aura, but a smattering of guilt stopped me. If we were friends, didn't he have a right to know I was invading his personal space? I rationalized it. It would be messy to explain, and I was in a tight spot, couldn't trust anyone, really. I scanned. The predominant silver hadn't changed. The pink had grown stronger, telling me he was serious about us having a friendship, but there were no warning signs in his energy field, no reason not to trust him.

I inhaled, long and deep, then planted my arse on the stool behind the counter. The silk draped with a swish over my legs and sent cool tingles of pleasure over my skin. I *needed* this dress. Maybe Jace was right about an allowance. "I'll speak to Hannah straightway, after Detective Stone clears my visitation rights."

A spark of amusement lit his eyes. "Good." He rubbed his thumbs over his fingertips, like it was a chore to keep from touching the fabric.

A woman could get lost in his touch. I was sure of it. Heat flashed along my nape, and I quickly waved toward the back of the store. "You might want to grab a stool from the dressing rooms. It isn't a short story."

By the time Jace settled, I'd gulped half my chai latte. He noticed the almost empty cup, and his lips kicked up at the corner. "I'm here to listen, not judge."

I started from the beginning and told him everything. It spilled out of me like water running through rapids.

Jace's eyes were dark green with a touch of brown—

his serious look. "So the only thing Thatcher's ghost said was 'witch?' Not which witch?"

"It was more like a shout, actually. It rather ping-ponged in my head for a bit, but he didn't say who. He didn't say anything, not in words like we're talking. It happened in my head." And that made me sound nutters for sure. I shifted on the stool. "What do you think he meant by it?" The latte churned in my stomach, because there could only be one answer.

Jace shook his head, then cranked out a strained laugh. "Hard to say. I've only met three witches in my life. And if that doesn't make me sound crazy, nothing will."

My interest piqued. "Who besides Hannah and me?"

"My father. Remember I told you he had sporadic attacks of clairvoyance."

"That sounds more psychic than witchy."

Jace nodded, then stood. "That's true, but from where I sit they're very similar in many ways. Will you be all right? I need to meet with a witness in a few minutes, but I'll be back to walk you home tonight."

The stubborn in me wanted to argue, to tell him I'd be just fine on my own. But it would have been a lie. "I'd appreciate that. But I have to do a reading before we leave. For Hannah." The words were sour on my tongue. "I have to be sure Thatcher wasn't accusing her."

A breeze lifted the hair off my neck.

I grabbed a handful of the loose strands, making a fist, then spun to face the front door. Closed.

Chapter 4

TWO OF PENTACLES

Tricky launch of a new project.
Juggling time and money.

WAS THATCHER HAUNTING OLA'S? "NOT OKAY."

Jace touched my cheek, and I turned to face him, putting the checkout counter between us. His eyes narrowed. "What's wrong, Cait? What's not okay?"

I attempted a smile. "Nothing. I forgot to tie my hair up this morning. I didn't realize until now." I twisted it into a knot, snatched a pencil from the container on the counter, and stuck it through the knot. "I'd best fix it before any more customers show up. See you tonight, then?"

"You're not getting away with that. I've told you before, you can't lie worth a damn."

It was true. "I always forget, and the words just tumble out before I can stop them."

His laugh sounded like gravel crunching—rich, full, and with a nice bite. "Talk to me, Caitlin."

I rubbed at the prickles on my neck. "A breeze. But there isn't one in here. I haven't propped the door open like Hannah does."

He shot a sideways glance at the door, then rested his gaze on me. "So it was a ghost?"

Was that what I thought? I shook my head. "Not exactly. I didn't see any energy ripples like those surrounding Thatcher's image during the clearing. It was more a premonition. A warning."

"Just before it happened, you said something about Thatcher accusing Hannah of his murder."

I nodded. "Yes. I want to do a Tarot reading for clarity about what he meant by witch. It could be a Wiccan, or maybe he was referring to a bitch."

"But?" Jace asked.

"But I'm ninety-nine percent positive he meant witch. And honestly, that single word was so vibrant compared to the nothingness of his visible form, I believe he was trying to tell me the killer was a *powerful* witch." Fear caught in my throat. "Like Hannah."

Jace reached over the counter, and tucked a loose curl behind my ear. "Or you."

My temper sizzled. "I did not—"

"I know you didn't. What I'm trying to say, and badly screwing up, is there might be more powerful witches out there than you and Hannah. It's our job to find out who they are, and how they're related to Thatcher."

A tiny grin worked its way free. "According to your fellow officer, also known as Hannah's former fiancé, we're supposed to have all the facts lined up *before* we come up with a theory. Sounds to me like you're working backwards, finding the killer before the motive. Not that I mind. It's the right way, probably the only way to get Hannah out of this mess."

Jace's mouth dropped open. "Nori gave you a lecture on forensic protocol? Sounds like him. A very by-the-book cop. I was too, still am, but an open mind goes a long way in successful law enforcement."

Something soft warmed my insides. "You have that, Jace. Both the strong foundation and an open mind. It means a lot to me that you accept my Wiccan abilities."

He tucked his chin, almost hiding a smile. "Grew up with it. Hard to deny. Will you share what it's like for you, being a witch?"

No one had ever asked me, and I wasn't sure how to describe it. "It's not like my cousin, Everly. She works in pure white energy, the sort most people attribute to *good* witches. Mine isn't like that. Not that I'd do anything harmful or bad, that isn't me at all. But my Wiccan genes are different."

"I guessed that. You're not like anyone I've ever met." His eyes sparkled, giving me the courage to continue.

"It's dark, or maybe not. It feels like outer space to me, which *looks* dark, but when you're in it, it's cool and the energy patterns are like crystal, clear and vibrant." I glanced at Jace, wondering if I was scaring him. He looked interested, focused on what I was saying, so I kept talking. "You know the depth of intensity you feel when you stare at the sky between the stars?"

"I've never thought of it, but yes. I get that." He smiled, sweet and gentle.

I fought the urge to lift his chin, and rub my thumb

over the smile. Maybe I could explain this after all. "I'm the opposite of Everly. The energy she uses to heal glows white and reflects all colors. Mine is dense because it absorbs all colors, which is why I call it inside-out. When I touch it, even just the edge, it's like being in that moment before time when everything was dark, silent, and still. I'm immersed in it, absorbed by it. It's a wee bit scary, Jace, which is why I'm so careful about using it." I shrugged, to ease some of the tension building in my shoulders. It was difficult to talk about this, to put voice to my innermost fears. "People usually refer to dark energy as occult or bad. Mine isn't like that at all. And it's not like earth power, either." I shrugged again. "It's just me."

He tipped his head to the side, and grinned. "Why don't we call it midnight energy? Don't you think that fits? Because it absorbs color, so you can work with energetic patterns like your cousin does, only from the reverse direction. She works with noon, you work with midnight. Have I got it right? Besides, it fits your hair."

Jace had identified it perfectly, and a tiny thrill danced over my skin. "Yes, midnight is exactly what it feels like, and it's not so scary if I think of it as being the opposite of lunch time. Like a late dinner. It's perfect. Thanks for...getting who I am."

He leaned over the counter and planted a kiss on my forehead.

My vision blurred. Holy crap, he kissed me. Like a friend, but it was still a kiss.

"Thank you, Cait. I'm honored you shared something so deeply personal with me." This time his smile flashed quickly, showing off the cheek-wink dimple that came out so rarely. "Stay out of trouble, Midnight. I'll be here when you read for Hannah tonight, so don't start without me."

"Okay. I..." He was gone. Disappeared out the door before I gathered my wits. He called me Midnight. Like it was a good thing to be.

FOR THE NEXT HOUR I focused on Ola Boutique work: straightening the displays, propping the door open, and helping several waves of customers. They were all nice, but it would have been so much easier if they didn't show up in bunches. The gaggles of women who flowed through the store seemed to be friends, or became friends while they tried on clothes and offered each other opinions about what looked good. As I'd never had enough cash to spare for fancy clothes, my learning curve was quite steep.

I kept up with the customers, but kept an eye on the Wiccan display case. No one approached it, or showed any interest whatsoever. It threw me, because after the appearance of Thatcher, I'd expected witches to show up at the store. At least one, so I could do a reading on a verified Wiccan person, someone besides Hannah, who could give me a baseline for comparison.

Disappointment squashed the pleasure left over from Jace's kiss, so when a quiet spell hit the boutique, I turned to the Tarot. I normally pulled a card for myself every morning, but preparing for the casting circle had messed me up something fierce, and it was time to get back to the basics of my Craft.

Whenever I touched the cards, a frisson of energy

flowed into me. I welcomed it, like connecting with the most important friend I had. They were my link to Universal energy. I shuffled longer than usual, just because I needed to feel them, to strengthen our bond, and my trust in how they spoke to me.

Eventually I cut the deck and selected a card. The Chariot. Diverse meanings sifted through my mind, and I jotted down some notes. Triumph. It was a good word, solid, and hopeful. Chariot was also a symbol for willpower, direction, movement, progress, and maybe most importantly for mind over matter.

I took them one at a time. Willpower was difficult, because I wasn't sure what it meant. Self-discipline for sure, and strength, but how did it apply to today? My first casting ate up a bunch of strength—seriously, it had drained me completely. But even before I started to create the circle, I'd called on the power of my Wiccan ancestors. I tucked the word away to consider again after I did Hannah's reading.

Direction. That one spiked my temper. Thatcher could have given me more to work with than a single word, and an open-ended one at that. I mean, witch meant a ton of different things. I made a note to come back to this, and drew another card for clarity.

I tapped the top of the deck. An explanation for this morning had to be here, but so far it was as confusing as Thatcher's unexpected appearance. Movement. That fit and definitely happened. The dead guy had floated in front of me like he had every right to take over my circle. He was a complication that made me late, so I had to jog home and rush through my shower. But I didn't see how any of those things would lead me to Thatcher's killer.

Frustrated, I circled progress. It looked so innocent sitting on my notepad, but was hardest of the four words to understand. Had I made progress? Yeah, but it wasn't the kind I'd wanted. Thatcher's "witch" condemned Hannah more than helped her. So why had it been the only word Thatcher said?

Patience wasn't even the tiniest part of my personality, but another thing The Chariot stood for was smooth transitions. Nothing had been smooth about this morning. Not the casting, not my time with Jace, and not dealing with customers. On the up side, maybe that meant this afternoon would be filled with all sorts of slick changes—like pinning down the murderer.

There was a promise of progress inherent in The Chariot, an implication that the driver—me in this case—had control. That I should feel confident, and stay focused on the task at hand. But there was something missing. I closed my eyes, imagined myself sitting high in a chariot, holding the reins, and snapping a whip above the horses. In a sense, I was doing just that by digging into Thatcher's life, investigating possibilities that weren't connected to Hannah.

With a sigh, I drew another card for clarity about what direction to take. Witch was a vague word at best, thoroughly irritating, and pointed to an entire sub-population of humans.

I turned the card over—Three of Wands.

I grinned. Success, vision, and opportunity. The Three

of Wands was a great card, full of hope and promise. It signaled major possibilities, a good time to plot my next move, and best of all that an opportunity was hanging out just waiting for me to trip over it. Which I fully intended to do.

A new group of shoppers flooded the store before I had a chance to put my cards away. One of them spotted the deck and gave me a huge grin. "Do you read?"

Sometimes the cards worked really, really fast. I scrambled for the right words to build on this opportunity. "Yes, I do. Are you interested in a session?"

She nudged the woman next to her. "Isn't her accent just precious? We both want readings, don't we, Lynn?"

Her companion nodded, clearly the shyer of the two.

I needed a calendar. And some bloody idea of what to charge. "I do readings in the evening, directly after the store closes. Does that suit you?"

They looked at each other, sharing some kind of silent communication, then the spokeswoman nodded. "Would tomorrow evening work for you?"

Excitement gushed through every pore of my being. "Yes, of course. I'll just make a note. Ola's closes at five, so if you could be here a few minutes after..."

They nodded in unison. Neither asked the price. I'd kept a running tally of sales in my head, not that I share the weird part of my brain that has an affinity for numbers with anyone, but I appreciated it. Made it ever so much easier to put a price on my services. Hannah was doing well with the boutique. Very well. "My readings take approximately forty-five minutes and are one hundred dollars."

"Perfect," the spokeswoman said without batting an eye. Then the two of them set about shopping with enough determination to pay Hannah's mortgage for the next few months. And after tomorrow night, I'd be able to make a fifty-percent payment on my new dress.

New rule: keep the Tarot deck visible at all times.

I slipped out from behind the counter to help the handful of customers who were sorting through racks of clothes and home décor displays, but stopped mid-stride when the phone rang. Surprise rippled under my skin. I'd been working for almost five hours, and it was the first time the shop telephone had sounded. It seemed odd, being a business and all, but Hannah's customers flowed in and out of the boutique like it was their second home, so maybe there was no reason for anyone to call. I snatched the phone off its stand. "Ola's Boutique."

"Ms. Connor."

My blood chilled at the sound of his distinctive voice. "Yes, Detective Stone."

"I've cleared a visit with Ms. Matthews for you. This evening. Six sharp." The dial tone buzzed in my ear.

I replaced the phone, my heart skipping against my ribs. In less than three hours I'd find out how Thatcher's blood got on Hannah's hands.

Chapter 5

EIGHT OF PENTACLES

Schedules and deadlines.

THREE HOURS BEFORE THE SHOWDOWN. OLA'S closed in two, which left very little time to get to the jail. Especially since I had no bloomin' idea where it was, and only the bus system for transportation. I glanced at the store full of customers. Nope, it would be a bad idea to ask for directions to the local nick. Might send them running for a different boutique, and that wouldn't do at all.

I would've asked Stone, but he'd hung up before I had a chance to gather my wits. The whole situation was all a-cock. And what about jail protocol? Were there things I needed to know, besides the obvious of not carrying weapons on my person? And I couldn't wear this dress to a jail. Totally inappropriate to show up as a Gypsy fortune teller. The shorts and grungy t-shirt I'd worn this morning were equally unfitting. Bollocks, I'd have to collect something else from Hannah's stock. It would have been quite a lovely turn of events if I had an unlimited income. But I didn't. And it wasn't.

I could ring Jace up, but didn't have his number. Oh!

But I'd gone completely daft. Jace would be here at five o'clock to keep tabs while I did Hannah's Tarot reading. He'd surely know where the jail was located, and about any pertinent protocol.

"Miss, could you help me, please?" It wasn't a request I could refuse, so I put on my shop girl face and went to work.

The next two hours flew by. The shop was filled with customers who kept me running—I *had* to buy some work slippahs—the entire time. It was good I didn't have time to dwell on my upcoming meeting with Hannah, but as I'd had no time to plan what to say, or how to ask about the blood, my nerves were totally rattled. And I still had to prepare a deposit slip for the day's take. Hannah was arrested before she had a chance to give me the particulars, but I'd managed a quick look at the process in her notebook. It wasn't at all difficult, except I didn't know the bank's location. And I *still* didn't have a mobile to look it up.

I managed to finish up with customers and shoo them away by ten past. The bank would hold until tomorrow, but I needed clothes, and Jace. I really needed Jace.

I snagged one of the Rag and Bone t-shirts, because I knew it would fit perfectly, and being white, would go with everything. The skirt had to do double duty: conservative enough for a jail visit, but still suitable for a Tarot reading Gypsy. I settled on a sleek cut skirt, full at the hem, and with an elastic waist that would make for an easy fit. It took thirty seconds for me to change, and slip my battered feet into the rubber flip-flops. They'd have to do.

Jace poked his head in the front door directly after I stepped out of the dressing room. "Readings require a wardrobe change?" he asked.

His comment surprised a soft laugh from me. "Oh, no. Not at all. I guess I thought Stone told you. I have to be at the jail to see Hannah in forty-five minutes. How far is it?"

He paled. "Rush hour traffic, and it's in downtown Honolulu. There's no way we'll make it by six."

Panic, frustration, and nothing but a short nap last night were my undoing. Tears brimmed, and trailed down my cheeks. "I have to get there. Stone was adamant about the time. Six sharp."

Jace palmed his mobile. "Let me try to—"

"No." I swiped at my tears, then grabbed his hand. "If you'll just ring Detective Stone, it's my responsibility to chat him up, see if I can get the visit switched."

Jace punched in some numbers, then handed me the phone. But he looked on, ready to step in if I needed help. I couldn't decide if his protectiveness suited me, or irritated me. Not surprising. I'd witnessed a few situations where Everly seemed to have the same difficulty with Tynan Pierce. It must be one of those male-female things.

The conversation with Stone went far better than I'd hoped, and we had things re-adjusted in no time. I ended the call with a smile.

"I'm surprised that went so well," Jace said, tucking his phone in his pocket.

"The Universe helped. Apparently there was an accident on the freeway, and Stone had already rescheduled our meeting for seven. We can make that, right?"

He nodded. "Yes, but we should leave now. If we get there early, we can grab something to eat. Okay with you?"

"More than. I haven't had a thing since the latte you brought me." Right on cue, my stomach gave an obnoxious grumble.

Like all cops do, Jace had scanned the shop when he

walked in, but now he did a double-take. "It's a mess, but I don't get how that stopped you from ordering lunch."

"Order..." I rubbed my fist over my painfully empty stomach. "I could have ordered food? How does that work? There's only OTB or Starbucks, and I couldn't leave the shop unattended to pick up an order."

His forehead wrinkled into adorable little lines. "They're closer than a football field. I'm sure someone would have delivered your lunch if you'd asked."

"It...I'm." Oh, bloody hell, I was a mess. "I haven't caught up to the learning curve of running a shop. When I worked as a server, we took turns eating in the kitchen. Food was always available."

"Come on," he said, taking my hand. "We can talk about arranging a one-person boutique schedule in the car."

I kicked my stubbornness aside and accepted Jace's help. I hadn't realized what a disaster the shop was until I noticed his shocked expression. There had been a steady stream of customers early in the day, but I'd managed to keep up with them. It wasn't until after I pulled my daily Tarot card that things went to shambles. So many customers had crowded into the shop at one time, and kept me busy asking questions about the Tarot, and ringing up sales, there'd been no chance for me to fold clothes or tidy the dressing rooms.

Exhaustion rested heavy on my shoulders. "I'll have to come in early tomorrow to put things back in order, but if you could show me where the Hawaiian Pacific bank is, it would be a big help."

"We'll drive by on our way to Honolulu. It's farther than your condo, but shouldn't take you more than twenty minutes or so to walk it."

Jace held the car door while I sat and arranged my

skirt. "Damn, but that's hot," I said, sucking in a breath. He'd parked in the sun, and the fabric seats had absorbed an uncomfortable bit of warmth. I lifted onto tiptoes to help lift my thighs away from the seat. Very awkward when seated.

Pink stained Jace's cheeks. "Sorry. I would have looked for a shady spot, but since I was late and thought we'd be in Ola's until after sunset..."

"It's fine. Should only take a few minutes to cool down."

He closed the door, circled around the back of the car, and slid behind the wheel. He was wearing shorts, and a bit of bare skin hit the seat. "Shit. That's really hot." Then he shot me an impish grin. "Maybe we should pick up some aloe lotion. I could help with hard-to-reach areas."

He deserved an eye roll for that, and I made sure he got one.

Chapter 6

EIGHT OF SWORDS

*Feeling powerless and
at the mercy of outside forces.*

IT TOOK US SLIGHTLY OVER AN HOUR TO REACH
Honolulu, which left about forty minutes before my visit
with Hannah. During the ride, Jace briefed me on protocol,
and confirmed that my new sundress would have been
unacceptable, as would my shorts. He also lectured me
about taking proper care of myself—as in eating on a
regular basis. It was another of those overprotective
moments that left me on the borderline of irritated and
quietly pleased, but I was too exhausted to decide which.

We made a quick stop at a street vendor for
hamburgers and sweet potato chips, and then it was time.
My muscles were tight with apprehension. Not only had I
never been inside a jail before, but I wasn't sure how
Hannah would react to my visit.

Razor wire lined the perimeter of the grounds. I don't
know what I expected, but there was something so very
final about those cold, lethally sharp edges. Jace walked
me to the door, our fingers laced as we crossed the parking

lot. I tightened my grasp when we reached the entrance, suddenly reluctant to let go. Maybe it was the aura of desperation clinging to the worn wooden bench outside the door, or maybe it was when I spotted a child's dirty dummy partly hidden behind one of the legs. "Families must wait out here." My stomach lurched.

Jace nodded. "Yeah, moms with kids."

Disturbing didn't begin to cover it. I pointed at the piece of faded blue plastic. "Someone lost their dummy."

"Their what?"

"Dummy. You know those rubber things babies suck on to quiet them."

He gave it another look. "Oh, you mean a pacifier."

I shrugged. "I think we might have a language disconnect."

"Could just be I'm not up on baby stuff." He sounded wary, unsettled.

"Men usually aren't." I reached for the door, but he beat me to it, and held it open.

"Thanks, Jace. You've made this easier."

"I'll be right here when you're ready to leave," he said, and those beautiful, ever-changing eyes looked bleak.

I breathed out a slow sigh, let go of his hand, and walked into the prison. It wasn't a regular visiting time, so I was the only person filling out the required forms to go through security. It was probably a good thing, since they weren't quite sure what to do with my UK identification. A quick phone call took care of that issue, and I moved on to the metal detector. A simple hurdle, because the only thing I carried with me was my British driver's license.

But the next bit wasn't easy at all. A tall, burly, stone-faced guard took custody of me, and piloted me down a hall to a double-locked steel door. He entered a passcode and then used a key. There was a faint grating sound when the door opened, as if it wanted to stay closed and not let anyone in or out. Anthropomorphizing a hunk of steel, even quietly in the back of my mind, probably meant I should be locked up somewhere safe. But not here. Not ever here.

Voices—a stifled scream, yelling, and, oh God, singing—closed in on me. Every hair on my body stood at attention, but the guard didn't so much as blink. When I flinched, he looked down on me with shuttered, condemning eyes that left no doubt he'd stuffed me in the same category as the prisoners.

The door closed behind us with a *thunk,* and the street-vendor cheeseburger gave serious consideration to making a reappearance. This was one of those unexpected moments that scarred a person for life. I had no idea my soul would rebel so completely at being incarcerated. And it was only for a short time. How was Hannah ever going to survive this?

A buzzer sounded. I jumped, my skin too tight. The guard didn't so much as hesitate in marching me along, as though the jarring noise hadn't just scared a dozen years off my life. He led me to a room with another locked door, but this one was equipped with only a simple keypad. After punching in the code, he pushed it open, and motioned me inside. "There's audio and video. I'll be right outside. Knock when you're ready to leave." The door closed behind him, shutting out the unnerving sounds of prison life.

Hannah stared at me wide-eyed, the normal silver shade of her irises replaced with dull, shadowed gray. A chill slithered under my skin. "Hannah," I whispered.

Handcuffed, sitting at an ugly institutional table, she simply wiggled her fingers at me in a parody of freedom. It crushed my heart.

I fought for a breath, inhaled the astringent odor of strong cleaning solution, and wondered what had happened in this room that required such intense scrubbing. I forced my legs to move, every step heavier than the last. The echo of my flip-flops slapping against the soles of my feet shredded the I'm-fine façade I'd so carefully created over dinner with Jace.

I made it across the room before my knees gave out, scraped the steel chair over the cement floor, and collapsed onto the cold metal—a startling contrast to the blistering heat of Jace's car seats. "I...don't know what to say. Only a tosser would ask how you are, because it's obvious..." I shook my head, shrugging. Bloody hell, my body didn't even know how to move in this place.

Hannah's smile was forced, but she gave it a good shot. "I'm okay, Cait."

"No, you're not. No one would be." I leaned toward her. "I'm doing my best to find the killer."

Her eyes dilated, black stealing the dismal gray. "Audio," she whispered.

My temper flared. "So how are we supposed to chat?" I reached to cover her hands with mine. Hell didn't break loose, so I figured touching her was allowed. "Is it okay? This?" I tightened my hold on her.

"Yes. But only in greeting, and then just before you leave. You should probably move back now. Brief touching to greet and say goodbye is allowed, since inmates are subjected to a body search after seeing a visitor."

Shivers hit the pit of my stomach. I had to get Hannah out of here, and that meant I had to ask questions, no matter how uncomfortable. I folded my hands in front of me, clearly visible to cameras, and then leaned close to her. "I need to know how Thatcher's blood got on your hands." I barely moved my lips, and spoke so softly audio shouldn't be able to pick up my voice.

"It's okay," Hannah said. "I've already talked with my attorney about it. I was at Ola's quite a while before you saw me, and had already found Thatcher's body and checked his pulse. There was so much blood on his neck, I...panicked. Wiped my hand off with a tissue, then tossed the evidence in the trash. Because I had a suspicious history with Thatcher, I ran and huddled in my car for the better part of an hour. When I saw you, the only thing in my mind was how desperately I needed an alibi. I'm sorry, Cait. It was wrong to use you that way, and it was a bad mistake."

A mishmash of thoughts and emotions tumbled in my brain, but one detail was certain. I would have done exactly the same dumb thing. "I get it."

Hannah tipped her head back, closed her eyes for a minute, then focused on me. "Detective Stone has seized my car, and is testing for Thatcher's blood." Tears pooled in her eyes. "I don't know if finding it will hurt or help my case."

"Maybe Jace will hear something. If the evidence corroborates your story, it should help, right?" I desperately wanted to give her hope, but only got a tiny nod of agreement.

"I have one more question. Do you know more witches? Local ones?" I didn't dare share my early morning experience with Thatcher's apparition, not with audio surveillance.

"Yes, there's a small coven on the North Shore. I don't belong, so don't know any of the *members* well, but I can give a list to Detective Stone. I'm not allowed to pass a note to a visitor."

Hannah's had emphasized members in a strange sort of way, but it was probably just stress, and there were more important things to ask her about. "Should I give any information I learn to your attorney? Who is he?"

"She. An old friend from high school. Naoko Kita. She might be able to help you find the people on the list I'll send you through Detective Stone. No, that's silly. If you're going to meet with her anyway, we can bypass Detective Stone, and I'll just give her the names."

Obviously Hannah didn't want to say "witches" aloud, and with the vibes in this place, I could see her point.

"Oh, I almost forgot. This is really embarrassing, but I don't have any clothes suitable for working at Ola's, and—"

She cut me off with a wave of her cuffed hands. "We're partners, at least for the time being. Please take whatever you need from the store. Ola's does very well, and can afford to supply you with a new wardrobe. It's the least I can do."

Humble gratitude poured through me. "Thanks. That's...I didn't expect you to donate clothes to my cause. I thought maybe an allowance. They're so pricey, um, for my budget anyway, and holy crap, that's an amazing gift, Hannah."

Her mouth curved in a slight smile. "You're welcome, but you're going to need to replace those rubber slippahs." She blew out a sigh. "I'm allowed phone privileges. We can keep in touch that way."

The first shred of happiness since I'd entered the prison warmed my heart. "Regular phone communication will be a huge help. I'll sign up for a plan, and buy a new phone tonight. There's probably a special number for inmates. If you add it to the list you're sending with your attorney, I'll ring you up—"

She shook her head. "I can only call out. Give your number to Naoko, and she'll get it to me."

I nodded. Hannah's skin had faded to a pasty gray shade. "I should probably leave, and let you...you probably don't get any rest here at all?"

"Not really. The noise is...disconcerting. But I have a meeting with Naoko tonight, and I should prepare for it. Oh, here's an idea. After you get your new number, why not leave a message for her at the front desk. That way she can give you a call and set up a meeting with you right away."

"Perfect. I'll chat up the guard at the desk, and fill him

in before I leave."

She blew out a soft sigh. "Thanks for doing what you can to prove my innocence. It helps me get through the days, knowing people care."

I gave her bound hands one last squeeze, and stood. "I need to get to a phone store before they close, or none of our plans will work out."

She attempted a shaky wave.

Without looking back, I rapped on the door, alerting the guard, and was ushered through the exit process. I stopped at the reception desk, and explained my plan to the woman behind the desk. She knew Naoko Kita by sight, had her on the visitor roster, and promised to pass along my message. That done, I stepped outside and into the evening breeze. It caressed me with its gentle touch, and my skin settled like it fit again.

Chapter 7

ACE OF WANDS

Breakthrough in thinking. Revelations and transcendent thoughts.

I FILLED JACE IN ABOUT THE BLOOD ON HANNAH'S hands and the North Shore coven. "Have you heard anything about a group of witches?" He probably would have told me, but there was no harm in double-checking.

He was quiet while we strolled across the parking lot. "No. I've been trying to find someone who might know about them, but I've got nothing so far."

Before we got in the car, he turned me to face him. "Are you all right? It can really fuck a person up in there. I remember my first time, and it turned into a six-pack night. Hard to get through the smells and sounds. They get inside you."

I dropped my forehead to his chest, and breathed in his scent before I lifted my head to meet his gaze. "I'll be okay. Everything you just said is right, and all the more reason we have to find the real murderer. I never understood prison suicide until tonight. It was bloody awful, Jace."

He tucked a loose strand of hair behind my ear. "Maybe we should stop someplace for a glass of wine before I take you home."

I shook my head. "No. I'm knackered, and wine messes with my sleep."

"The offer's open, Cait. If you ever need to talk about it."

Right on cue, the waterworks threatened, just like they always did when someone was nice to me. "Thanks," I mumbled, backing away from him to hide the tears flooding my eyes. "I'll remember."

We were in the car and on our way when I explained about the deal with Hannah's attorney. "I need to buy a phone tonight. Hannah said she can call me, and I suppose I could use the boutique phone, but I'd rather not talk to her from there." I shrugged. "I don't have a good reason, it just doesn't feel right. But I need one tonight so I can leave the number with the guard manning the reception desk. Can we stop at a mobile store?

"Sure can. I want you to have your own cell, too, so you can call me if you get into trouble. There's a Verizon store not too far away, and they're open until nine. We can make it with a few minutes to spare."

In less than thirty minutes I was the happy owner of a new iPhone, complete with internet connection and an email address. I immediately rang up the prison and left the message for Hannah's attorney, and on the ride back to the North Shore, I happily created my contact list. "Okay. I have Aunt Nolla, you, Everly, the prison reception desk, and the Ola Boutique numbers listed." As I read them off, I realized it was a damn sparse list of friends, and two of them weren't even human. "I can add Naoko when she rings me up."

Jace shot me a sideways glance. "Naoko Kita is Hannah's attorney?"

"Yes. Is that good?" I asked, yawning. My curiosity was the only thing keeping me awake.

"Better than. She's the best, and is particular about the cases she accepts. Hannah is damn lucky to have her."

"Hannah said they went to high school together." I stifled another yawn. "That might have influenced her to take the case."

Jace nodded. "Had to have helped." He paused a beat. Two. "About your contact list. Will you humor me and add the number for Uncles: OTB, please? At least I'll know you won't starve while you're at work."

My mind was getting foggy with exhaustion, but through the mushiness, I realized Jace had made a good point, and it was...endearing. "Do you know it? Their number?"

Jace rattled it off like the restaurant was his best friend. "You must eat there often," I said, punching the number into my new phone. My eyes drifted closed.

It was too dark to see, but I sensed his blush. "I once dated a server who worked there."

Something fluttered in my chest, and I was suddenly alert. Holy crap was that jealousy? About a man I'd known all of two days? I'd lost it, gone totally 'round the bend. "You called her at work?" Oh, double crap. Now I even sounded jealous.

Jace's grin sparkled white in the oncoming headlights. "She was like you, with no phone. Only way to reach her was to leave messages with the hostess. It didn't work out."

"You don't sound upset about it." I was poking where I didn't belong, and the only thing shutting me up was holding back the yawns taking over my ability to speak. Damn, but I was knackered.

"As you would say, we didn't suit."

Jace had mangled his imitation of my British-Irish-Scottish accent, and for the first time all day I let out a genuine laugh. It warmed my insides. I gave him a feeble punch in the arm, because it was second best to kissing him senseless. And that would be a bit premature, plus I wanted to be more awake when it happened.

My phone rang when we were almost back to the North Shore, and jarred me awake, my nerves buzzing with anticipation. "It has to be Naoko, right?"

Jace just shook his head. "My best guess says you're right."

Naoko's voice was strong, clear and kind, nothing at all like Dobney, and I liked her right off. We'd quickly made arrangements to meet at Ola's the next morning at nine o'clock, and she rang off so as not to be late for her meeting with Hannah. I skimmed the tip of my finger over the slick surface of my new phone. "Naoko had a ten o'clock meeting scheduled on the North Shore tomorrow, and is going to fit me into her schedule just before that. We only talked for a minute, but I have a good feeling about her, Jace."

"Um-hmm," he agreed. "I've watched her in court a few times, and if I were accused of murder, she'd be my first phone call."

"I think that's probably the best recommendation Hannah could have." And for the first time since I tripped over Thatcher's shoe, I had hope that everything would work out. I curled into the bucket seat, my thoughts drifting into oblivion.

When Jace grabbed his phone out of the cup holder, I startled awake. We were parked in front of my condo, and I'd totally missed most of the ride home. Embarrassment flooded my cheeks. Should I ignore it? Maybe he hadn't noticed I'd been sleeping.

"What's your new number?" he asked, a smidgeon of laughter in his voice.

I rattled it off while he punched it into his mobile. "We're all set. I'll walk you to the door, Cait, and I should plan on being at Ola's...when?"

"You mean for Hannah's Tarot reading? The one I didn't have a chance to do this evening?"

"Yeah, you nodded off a few times on the drive home, and were sound asleep when we got to Ola's. I didn't stop, figuring you'd want to be fresh and awake to do the reading. Was I wrong?"

Oh, pisser. I'd *really* hoped he hadn't noticed. "No, it was very considerate. Sorry I fell asleep. It wasn't the company."

"I get it. I'm always exhausted after a jail visit."

It made sense, what with the huge emotional drain, and my heart did a funny flutter. "You understand me, what I'm going through. It means a lot, Jace." It took me a minute to bite back the flood of emotion, and to stop tears before they leaked out, but I got myself under control. Damn, it was difficult when people were nice to me. I cleared my throat. "I need to tidy up the shop first thing, and then meet with Naoko. I think it would be best to do the reading right at four. I scheduled two readings with Ola customers at five, so I'll just have to close the shop early. I hate to do it, but really there's no choice. Will that work for you?"

"Works well. I have to be at the Honolulu PD for three sketches tomorrow, but I'll be free by three, so will miss the rush hour traffic getting back here. Timing should be good."

I opened the car door, not sure how to say goodbye gracefully. "Okay. See you tomorrow. And thanks for today."

"Hold on." He flung the driver's door open, and jogged around the rear of the car. "I'll walk you home like my momma taught me."

A properly feminist woman would probably have waved him back to the car and then hurried off on her own. But I wanted the company. At least until I was sure neither Kahuna Aukele nor Thatcher's apparition were lurking inside. "I'd appreciate that, Jace. It's been a long day."

I JOLTED AWAKE WHEN MY new phone let out a jarring noise that sounded suspiciously like military trumpets. That would have to be changed as soon as I woke up enough to focus. I stumbled into the shower, took time to dry my hair because I couldn't pull off two wet hair days in a row, and dressed in the same shorts and t-shirt I'd worn yesterday. I'd select enough work clothes to mix and match for a week when I got to the shop.

The morning was cool enough for me to jog, so I stopped at Starbucks for a chai latte. Alana, my favorite barista, beamed at me from behind the counter. "You want me to add an oatcake to that, yah?"

Her smile was just what I needed to start the day, and since I'd jogged to work, an oatcake would be just the thing. "Yes, please. You remember me?"

"We don't get that many Brits stopping in," she said, handing me a bulging paper bag. Oatcakes were thick. And good. "That'll be seven-seventeen, please."

I picked up a customer rewards card, handed it to her with my Barclay Visa, and sighed. I'd have to see about getting a local bank soon. "Put fifty dollars on this, please. Looks like I'll be collecting breakfast here every morning, and having a card will be easier for both of us."

By the time Alana finished ringing me up, my latte was ready. "See you tomorrow," I said, then took a tentative sip of the piping hot drink.

Ola's looked dismal in the early morning light. I'd need to fix that right after I got yesterday's mess set to rights. Putting things away turned out to be a comforting job, and gave me a chance to learn about Hannah's inventory. The clothes and home décor items were fun to work with, and it was especially nice to select several skirts and tops for my own wardrobe. I dressed in a printed scarf skirt with a flowy, uneven hem, and flared white t-shirt, and then danced around the shop to watch the skirt swirl around my legs. The dancing was working wonders to chase my morning crankiness away...a good thing since I wanted to be in top form for my meeting with Naoko.

But the moment came to an abrupt end when the thong ripped out of my flip-flops. The mishap pushed shoe shopping to the top of my priority list, and a flutter of apprehension lodged in my stomach. It was rude to meet with an attorney barefoot. Even in the laid-back atmosphere of the North Shore, that couldn't be an acceptable practice. There was nothing for it, so I tossed the useless shoes into the trash, and for the next thirty minutes concentrated on balancing the cash drawer. I'd need to make a trip to the bank. "Why didn't I ask Hannah how she managed errands during the day, what with her being the only person to see to customers?"

My question hung lonely in Ola's early morning quiet. The shop needed...peaceful excitement. I selected a Barr-Co. candle from the home décor display, lit it, and then set it on a shelf behind the checkout counter. Perfect. The scent was clean and fresh. That done, I considered filling the metal tub with ice and arranging bottles of juice like Hannah had done the day I met her, but since there was no ice in the shop I figured she must have a machine in the storage area. Where Thatcher had been killed. And I hadn't thought to check if it was still cordoned off as a crime scene.

A shudder traveled down my spine. Surely there was a way for me to avoid ever needing anything from the storage area. I immediately shoved the idea of a juice display into the not-in-this-lifetime section of my brain, and not a moment too soon.

Naoko Kita rapped on the door, at least I assumed that's who it was. Fortunately Ola's had a glass panel, so there was never any doubt who stood on the other side. This morning it was a graceful Asian woman with sleek black hair and amber eyes. Her aura was pulsing in a steady rhythm, and it was the brightest blue I'd ever seen. I had a hard time pulling my gaze away to take in the excellent fit of her lightweight gray suit...and heels. I almost didn't open the door. There was no way to hide my bare feet, because the handkerchief hem on my new skirt hit at mid-calf.

My new motto: when in deep shit, try distracting them with a dazzling smile.

I barely got the door open before she offered her hand. "I'm Naoko Kita, and you must be Caitlin Connor."

"Yes," I said, shaking her hand. "Please come in." I locked the door behind her, and then led her to the checkout counter where I'd arranged a stool on either side. "Hannah said she'd give you a list of names for me, women who belong to a local coven."

Naoko handed me a slip of paper with six names printed in block letters. "Are you planning to interrogate these women, Caitlin?"

It was a fair question, since Hannah's defense was her responsibility. "I honestly don't know. Whatever I do has to be subtle. I'm not trained to face off with a murderer, but I am a witch." It wasn't a lie. And really there was no reason to mention that I *had* faced off with a murderer. And won.

"That may give you an *in* an undercover police officer wouldn't have, but I can't, would never, recommend that you approach these women. Hannah believes it's quite possible one of them murdered Ted Thatcher."

"I agree with her. Has she shared that possibility with Detective Stone?"

Naoko crossed her legs. "I don't believe so."

I shrugged. "It probably wouldn't help her case. I don't have any personal experience with covens, but I've read some things. They're...particular about who they talk to. At least that's my understanding. And Detective Stone is a bit intimidating."

We shared knowing smiles. "He can be," Naoko said, and handed me her business card. "Don't hesitate to call me if you have any questions, and please do contact me if you learn anything that might help Hannah's case."

"I will." We both stood, and headed toward the door. I had one more question, but hesitated to ask.

I'd unlocked and opened the door before I found the courage. "Hannah seemed frail when I visited. Understandably so, but is she going to make it through this, do you think?" The last bit came out in a rush.

Naoko was silent for a moment. "Yes. Hannah is a strong woman, a survivor, but she'll never be quite the same."

"Oh, I almost forgot." She tapped her phone, checked the time, then glanced at my bare feet and grinned. "Hannah said you needed shoes, and you don't have to open the store for another half hour. Come on, I'll take you to meet my uncle. He's a leather worker and makes all my slippahs."

"But..."

Naoko took a firm grip on my elbow, and steered me to her car. "It's just up the road, but he doesn't offer his work to the public, so you'll need me to vouch for you."

I was buckled into the passenger side of her Prius before I found my voice. "You didn't give me a chance to grab my duffle, and I don't have my credit card or any cash."

"Pfffft. Uncle Akinori does this for pleasure, and trust me, you won't walk out with a pair of shoes unless he decides you're worthy of his craft." She gave me a sideways grin. "Like some witches I know. Which reminds me, I'd like to schedule a Tarot reading with you."

Naoko was a powerful bundle of female energy, but I was determined to hold my own. "I charge. One hundred a reading."

Her laughter was full-bodied and utterly delightful. I liked this woman. A lot.

I left Uncle Akinori's shop with two pair of slippahs, and one pair of fabulous sandals that laced up my leg. I wanted to wear those for something special. Maybe I'd ask Jace out on a date, a real one that didn't involve murder or jails.

Chapter 8

SEVEN OF WANDS

Courage, determination, and creative thinking.

JACE STROLLED INTO OLA'S SHORTLY AFTER FIVE, A cardboard cup holder in his hands. "Evening. I thought we'd need caffeine to get through Hannah's reading," he said in greeting when I opened the door. "Did you get some lunch?"

It had been hours, and a few thousand dollars in sales, since my last taste of a caffeine-laden beverage, much less lunch. I grabbed the plastic cup from the holder with a firm tug. "Not exactly lunch, but Alana brought me a fruit parfait during her break. And now you've showed up with iced chai. It's perfect, what with the temperature in the nineties today, but how did you know?"

A mischievous smile touched his lips. "Alana suggested it, so I can't take any credit. She's taking good care of you. I like that. Shop looks good. Are you ready to start the reading?"

"I am." And then I remembered I hadn't selected a card for myself. It was the second day in a row I'd forgotten the importance of beginning my day with quiet time to reflect on the Tarot. But now it would have to wait until after Hannah's reading. I slipped the cards from their velvet pouch, and began to shuffle.

Before I laid down the first card, I took a huge swallow of my icy cold drink, and drew in a breath. It didn't help to calm me at all. "I really want to find some good news in this reading. Hannah needs it, and so do I."

Jace had pulled up one of the dressing room stools, and rested his elbows on the counter. "Yeah. Stone is diligent, and as solid a detective as I've ever worked with, but even he needs something to go on besides the captain's insistence that Hannah is guilty."

"So much hinges on this reading. I admit to being a little desperate for clues as to what to do next, and I really hope the cards will give me some clarity." I stopped fidgeting with the deck and looked at Jace. "I asked for guidance about Hannah's current situation with Ted Thatcher. Do you think it was a good question?"

He laid his hand over mine. "I think you have to trust your gut."

Not so easy with Hannah depending on me to find the real killer. "I'm going to do my favorite spread. It's five cards, and they represent the sun, dawn, noon, dusk, and midnight. The first position, and center card, is the sun. It will bring the hidden aspects of Hannah's situation to light."

"Hey, Midnight. That last card could be important 'cause it matches your energy, right?"

The *rightness* of it left me breathless for a minute.

"Yes, and it signifies the resolution of the issue. I better not think about it yet 'cause it's kind of messing with my head." Midnight. Me. I planted it firmly in the back of my mind, and carried on.

The Ten of Pentacles, reversed. "Usually this card has a hidden aspect, and has to do with the loss of financial security, but I've seen the books for Ola's, and it's a strong and viable business. The Ten of Pentacles reversed can also indicate family conflict or a hazardous adventure. From your friendship with Officer Nori, and knowing Hannah, is there anything you remember about a family conflict?"

"Only that Hannah broke their engagement. I'm thinking the wedding would have been hazardous if they'd gone through with it."

My memory buzzed. "Did you say Hannah broke the engagement? Officer Nori told me he did, because of her being a witch and all."

Jace shook his head. "Scuttlebutt has it she all but threw the ring at him when he asked her to give up her Wiccan way of life."

Progress, and we were only on the first card. "So the hidden aspect is Hannah refusing to give up her heritage. Does that sound right to you?"

"It's the truth, so we should probably go with it."

I made a note, and drew the next card. "This represents dawn, and will show us the situation that's manifesting." The Priestess, reversed. "That's two reversed cards, but the situation is ugly, so it fits. I just want to go on record as saying I don't like it, especially since this is a major arcana card."

Jace smiled. "Noted. I'm guessing upside down means she's evil personified, right?"

"Yes, and it fits perfectly with the reading I did yesterday, when the reversed Queen of Swords came up. She's evil, and think this might mean that if the killer is a witch, she might have lost touch with her Craft." I tapped the card. "I'm not sure, but maybe the rest of the reading will help to clarify it."

"Next," Jace said, prodding me to choose the next card.

"This is noon, and represents issues that cannot be ignored. I'm hoping it tells us exactly where to look for clues." I laid down the Queen of Wands. "Holy crap, it's another reversed card. There's a reason I usually only read cards in the upright position, but this time I thought it was important to consider the negatives as well as the positives."

"What's it mean?" Jace asked. He sounded calm, but he was rubbing his fist over his mouth, worrying his lips. It wasn't a typical reaction for him, at least not one I'd seen in the two days I'd known him.

"A sharp-tongued woman. It can be interpreted as anger that makes a person judgmental and suspicious, blaming others for a situation." A slight case of the dizzies hit me, and I scooted onto the stool Hannah kept behind the counter. "This fits with an evil female killer, possibly a witch, and Officer Nori wanting Hannah to give up her magic. There's a definite theme here."

I quickly pulled the next card. "This is dusk, and will tell us about any help Hannah will receive."

Jace leaned over, reading the card. "The Hermit."

I blew out a sigh. "At least it's not reversed. The only hermit-like person I've met here is my cousin Everly's grandfather, Kahuna Aukele. Maybe this means we should ask him for help."

Jace straightened up, staring at me. "The Kahuna is a legend around here. Always shows up where he's needed, always when you least expect him, and there's no way to contact him. He's *related* to you?"

"Only by a dotted line. Everly's father and mine were brothers, but Aukele is Everly's mother's father. Do you think I should ask him for help?"

Jace let out a snort. "Like I said, no one knows how to contact him. Your best bet would be to use your Craft to summon him." He snapped his fingers. "You know, that might work. He's an enigmatic old guy."

Nobody had to tell me *that*. "Okay. Let's put it aside for now. This is the last card, midnight, and it represents the resolution of the situation." I laid down the Two of Wands. Reversed. "Bloody hell."

"What?" Jace asked, leaning away from the card like it might bite him. He wasn't far off.

"Dread, pessimism, delays, decisions made before the facts are in and that could cause harm. It's a crappy card." The chai churned in my stomach.

Jace cocked his head to the side, and squinted at me. "If Hannah were here, and you were reading for her, what would you do right now?"

The answer came without thought. "Select another card for clarity."

He gave me a palms-up.

Determined to make this work in our favor, I picked up the cards. "How can we fix the negative outcomes?" I asked, then looked at Jace. "Ready?"

"Yeah. As ready as a guy can get when there's not a damn thing he can do to fix the situation." There was more than a little frustration in his voice.

"Your part comes in when the action starts." I turned over The Magician, laying it crossways on top of the Two of Wands. My throat landed somewhere around my navel. "Well. I'm not sure what to do with this."

"Talk me through it," Jace said. The man gave good backup.

"Talent and intelligence. The magician is independent, intuitive, and powerful. His talent carries responsibility." The words stuck in my throat. "I think it's me, Jace. He's also a trickster, and...that part reminds me of my midnight energy. Hannah doesn't have anything dark in her aura at all, but you know how my aura *looks* dark. There's a web of midnight strands holding all my light together. It's alive and vibrant, like a fast-running stream under a layer of ice."

"Why do you think it's you? This is Hannah's reading, so it could be her intelligence and Wiccan ability that will get her out of this mess." Jace: the voice of reason.

I drew in a long breath. "That makes sense. And it's true. But I'm positive this card represents me being in Hannah's life. I could feel my crazy DNA go wonky when I laid this card down, Jace. That doesn't happen to me very often."

"Okay," he said. "Let's go with that. What's your next step?"

I stared straight into those ever-changing eyes of his, dipped into the deep, rich teal of them, and knew without a doubt what I had to do. "I'm going to join the coven."

An it harm none.

The Moon

Caitlin's Tarot: Episode 3

She stands for truth and justice...

Hannah is still in jail. The person who killed Ted Thatcher is still at large. And Caitlin is determined to track down the real killer, even if it means she has to join a coven.

Officer Jace Porter believes in Hannah's innocence and wants to help Caitlin, but getting involved puts him in the uncomfortable position of butting into a forbidden case— one his captain considers closed.

Determined to discover the truth, Caitlin learns to use her gifts in unexpected ways, and when she's forced to confront hidden evil, she begins to accept the true beauty of her midnight energy.

It's only a matter of time before Caitlin will need to unleash her power to balance the scales of justice.

Chapter 1

SIX NAMES, AND EACH ONE A POTENTIAL MURDERER. I ran my finger over the delicate script Hannah had written, hoping one of them would feel different, would stand out in some way. No luck. There wasn't so much as a witchy tingle attached to any of them. The paper was heavy, and a rich cream color, nothing like I would expect the prison to have had on hand...which meant Hannah's attorney, Naoko Kita, must have provided it when they met the night before.

After Naoko delivered the list to me, she'd taken me, at Hannah's request, to visit her Uncle Akinori. He personally hand crafted sandals, and I had been in desperate need of some shoes. I left his cottage with four pairs, all butter-soft, but still strong enough to hold up in Hawaii's sudden rainstorms and exposure to the ever-present salt water and sand. I'd been wearing my favorite pair ever since, and kept wiggling my toes against the smooth leather, delighting in the satiny texture and perfect fit.

Those touches of normal kept my Wiccan life in balance.

On our way to Akinori's home, Naoko had hinted her uncle wouldn't give his handcrafted sandals to anyone unless they were worthy of his talent—unlike some witches she knew. It was a pointed reference, so of course I questioned her about it, but had gotten nothing in return but a change of subject. She wasn't on Hannah's witch-list, and because they'd been friends since childhood, I figured it wasn't an oversight. Naoko probably wasn't a practicing witch.

Which led to the question: how did she know any witches by name? I shrugged it off as being part of her job as an attorney. She might work with coven members as clients, so would be bound by client-attorney privilege.

Since talking with Naoko, I'd done some research on covens, and learned that member names were almost always kept private. Secret. I shivered. Secrets could be dangerous, especially if they hid a murderer. And with my new knowledge, I had to wonder how Hannah had learned about the six witches she listed. Not that it mattered. I *would* find a way to locate them. Hannah's freedom depended on it.

The trick would be to make myself interesting, someone they wanted to have in their group. Apparently covens were invitation-only gatherings, so it wasn't a simple matter of filling out an application. First thing on my to-do list: I had to befriend one of these women, and since Ola's carried supplies for the Craft, I had high hopes there would be a clue in the stack of credit card receipts Hannah hadn't yet filed with her accountant.

I made it to the shop two hours before opening, stopped to grab my usual *venti* chai latte and oatcake from Starbucks, and settled into one of the boutique's two overstuffed chairs. No point perching on a hard wooden stool when I was already faced with a tiresome task.

It took me an hour to separate out the receipts listing Wiccan supplies because I read each one thoroughly before dividing them into piles. That done, I stood and stretched, tossed my empty cup into the trash, and stowed the non-Wiccan receipts to pass on to the accountant. After spreading the remaining twenty-five possibilities on the counter, I sorted for repeat names, and came up with four.

Grabbing a blank sheet of paper from the printer tray, I wrote Potential Suspects across the top and underlined it three times. When I compared the four customer names who had purchased Craft supplies with Hannah's list, I didn't find any matches, but one of them had shopped at Ola's a few days before Thatcher was murdered. I moved her name to the top of the list, but couldn't eliminate any of the others.

Tucking my hair behind my ears, I worked up a fresh wave of enthusiasm, and sifted through the other receipts, comparing them to the names on Hannah's list. No one matched.

I plopped down on the wooden stool, braced my elbow on the counter, chin in hand, to consider the situation, but was delightfully interrupted when Jace

Porter rapped on the boutique door.

My heart did a skip-hop of happiness. Jace was a good chap, and knowledgeable about police business, so an excellent ally for me. Besides, I liked him, as in *really* liked him. I hurried to unlock the door with such a stupid-big grin on my face that it stretched my muscles. "Hi." It was the best I could do, 'cause the intensity of his ever-changing eye color left me awestruck. It was a phenomenon I wanted to ask him about, but the time hadn't been right yet.

"Hey, Midnight. Thought I'd follow up on your announcement yesterday about joining a coven." Tiny lines were etched around his lips. Was he worried about me?

"I'm working on it right now," I said, locking the door behind him. I loved that he'd started calling me Midnight, because it reminded him of my inside-out, mutant-DNA, witchy energy. It was a subtle bond between us that reinforced his acceptance of who I am, and made me want to be...better, stronger, more capable in my Craft. I sighed, content, until the morning's failure crept in on my thoughts. "So far I don't have any solid leads on who the murderer is, but I've collected a few more names of potential witches to check out. Too bad witchcraft isn't one of those activities law enforcement keeps running track of, like drug addicts and the like."

He flashed me a grin. "I asked around about a coven, but got nothing. This group must stay way under the local radar."

"It isn't surprising, I guess. Witchcraft isn't illegal, but

my research indicates that practitioners are private sorts."
I led the way back to the counter where I'd spread out the
receipts and handed him a stack. "Will you take a look at
these? Maybe a name will stand out, what with you being
local and all. They're all strangers to me."

Jace thumbed through the stack, pulled one out, and
frowned. "Ebba Deforest. Sounds familiar, but I'm not sure
why."

I plucked the receipt from his hand. "It's a starting
place."

"What did she buy?" Jace asked. "Might be helpful to
know."

"Um..." I scanned the receipt. "Holy crap. An athame.
One like Hannah's." My stomach took a nosedive.

"The murder weapon?" He voiced the words carefully.

"Yes. I recognize the SKU number because Detective
Stone asked about the one on display. He even had me
take it out of the case so he could study it more closely." I
double-checked the date on the receipt. "Ebba Deforest
purchased this one six days before Thatcher was killed."
Foreboding crawled down my spine.

Jace scrubbed his hand over his face. "Hang on. You've
got that look."

"What look?" I asked, making my eyes as big and
innocent as possible.

"Like you're about to chase her down and accuse her
of murder. Which is a bad idea, Midnight. That kind of
thing could get you arrested right along with Hannah."

"Not if I'm careful." I wasn't *planning* to threaten her
or anything, but we were definitely going to have a chat,

no matter how much it worried Jace. "I'll just pretend I'm thinking of buying an athame like her new one, and ask her how she likes it. That should be safe enough. And maybe she knows something about the coven, even if she's not a member."

"I've noticed subtlety isn't your strong point." He gave me a flicker of a smile.

"True. But I have to start some place. I could just give the list to Detective Stone, but what if he's too busy to chase down unsubstantiated leads?"

Jace shifted uncomfortably. "Captain put him on another case. Word is he doesn't want Stone to waste any more time on Thatcher's homicide. That doesn't mean Stone wouldn't follow up on your list, but with the captain convinced Hannah is guilty, he would have to do it in his free time. Cops don't get much of that."

I planted my hands on my hips. "My only other option would be Naoko, but she got weird about it when we talked about the list." Bending, I grabbed the phone book from under the counter and flopped it open. "Deforest. There can't be too many, since the majority of people living here are Asian or Hawaiian."

Jace paced. "At least meet with her in a well-populated place."

"Sure. No reason I can't do that." I ran my finger down the Ds. "Here it is, and there's only one. I'll ring her up straightaway," I said, punching the number into my new mobile.

Jace caught my hand. "Make sure you meet in a place where my presence will be inconspicuous."

"What? You don't have to be there. Shouldn't be, considering the coven is probably all female."

His stare singed my bones. "This isn't about the coven. It's about one woman who purchased a dagger identical to a murder weapon. I *will* be there."

And didn't that just throw a spanner in the works.

Chapter 2

TWO OF SWORDS

Armed peace. Uncertainty.

EBBA DEFOREST LIVED ON THE OPPOSITE END OF THE North Shore from me, which meant I was semi-dependent on Jace for transportation. A car was totally beyond my budget, so I grudgingly accepted his decision to go with me. Ebba had answered her phone before the first ring completed, and sounded composed, as though she'd been expecting my call. I used the plausible story about her new athame, the one I'd shared with Jace. The only thing I didn't do was insist on a public meeting place, but that was only because she hung up before I had a chance to suggest an alternative.

He was furious. Stomped around Ola's for a solid two minutes, which wouldn't have been a long time except for the lethal glares he kept shooting in my direction. I hadn't exactly clocked his pacing, but I continuously checked my new mobile to avoid eye contact, and had counted one hundred and twenty seconds.

They passed in brutally slow motion.

In a fleeting moment of panic, I even considered asking if he'd ever used his weapon in the line of duty—just as a heads-up. But when I scanned his aura, there was only a slight tinge of red sparking through the normal silver. There would have been a lot more if he was considering offing me. At least, I hoped there would be.

He came to an abrupt stop in front of the checkout counter. "Here's the compromise. You'll keep your cell phone on while you're in her house so I can listen to everything that goes down."

It was a decent bargain. "I can do that. We're supposed to be there at half one, so when do you want to pick me up? I hate having to close Ola's for the afternoon, but this information could be critical to ensuring Hannah's innocence."

He nodded. "Uh-huh. I'm guessing half one is actually one-thirty?"

"Right." I just wasn't getting the hang of American-speak at all yet.

"I'll be here at twelve-thirty," Jace said, a touch of steel in his voice. "I want to recon Deforest's neighborhood before you go inside."

"I'll be ready." No point quibbling over unimportant details, and if I closed Ola's at noon, I'd have enough time to grab an avocado and some cheese from the local convenience store, eat, and then freshen up before Jace arrived.

He gave me a quick nod, then spun around and stomped out the door.

I blew out a long sigh of relief, yanked my athame out

of my duffle, and began a clearing ritual to chase away Jace's anger. I drew a pentacle for each of the four quarters—east, south, west, and north. To ensure the protective sphere was all-encompassing, I sketched one above while I chanted: "Cleanse this space and make it clear, all joy and peace may it embrace." Then I completed the ritual by drawing a pentacle below while chanting: "Infinite power of the Divine, protect and bless this space through time. So mote it be."

The energy in Ola's immediately settled, so I tucked my athame away and took out my Tarot cards. I had just enough time for my daily draw before I had to open Ola's for business. A sensation of peace always streamed through me when I touched my cards, and this morning was no exception. I shuffled, cut the deck, and turned the top card over. The Moon. It was going to be a major arcana day.

First I focused on the symbolism of the artwork. Beams of light shining down on water, which represented the subconscious. I'd be working with intuition, empathy, and illusion today. There were shadows from the Moon that showed, or maybe caused, shifting shapes. This card could indicate strange encounters, and sensitivity to unseen forces, but more importantly I would need to remain on guard against deception.

I shuffled my cards and set them aside while I considered the upcoming meeting with Ebba Deforest. Shifting shapes and possible deception were a fair warning that things might not be exactly how they seemed. I checked the time—ten minutes before I needed to flip over the Open sign and unlock the store.

There was one more thing I wanted to do. I hurried across the store to the Wiccan display case where Hannah had stocked a lovely assortment of pentagram necklaces. I figured drawing the Moon was a sign I needed a talisman for luck—silver to symbolize lunar and psychic energy. The large and medium-sized pentagrams didn't spark so much as a tingle in my aura. I was about to ditch the idea of adding a piece of jewelry to my possessions, but spotted a necklace that had fallen between the end of the shelf and the side of the display case. I worked the leather cord free, then placed the pentagram in the palm of my hand. It had been crafted on a purple ceramic tile—so different from my midnight energy. It was a long way from the silver I'd thought I needed, but this one came from clay, from the earth, and radiated a cool, deep vibration that I was immediately drawn to. It was mine. I slipped it over my head, and with a grin opened the Ola Boutique for business.

JACE ARRIVED TO PICK ME up at precisely twelve-thirty, and we were on our way before I had a chance to catch my breath. "You're speeding."

He glanced at the speedometer. "Nope, just riding the limit."

The meeting with Ebba Deforest wasn't going to work unless Jace and I talked through our disagreement. "I understand, and agree, that my meeting with an unknown witch *should* take place in a public area, Jace, but you didn't hear our conversation. Her tone and word choice left no doubt our meeting had to be on her terms. Yes, she sounded interested in talking with me, excited even, but only if she held home court."

Jace sighed. "I understand, but I don't like it. You know I grew up with a clairvoyant dad, and I watched how that kind of power can go wrong. My dad was careful, but there were still repercussions when he shared what he'd seen with friends who didn't understand. He finally stopped talking to all of us, just bottled everything up. It scarred him *and* our family. I don't want that to happen to you, and we don't know a damn thing about this woman's gifts. You're going in blind, Midnight."

That's where he was wrong. "Not blind. I'll scan her before I approach the house, and Jace, you know I have a bit of power myself. I respect your concern. It's lovely, thoughtful, and not something I want to lose. But can you understand I need you to respect my ability, too? I'm a real witch. You've not seen much of my power, and I hope you never do, but..."

He grinned, flashing his dimple. "We've only known each other two days, three counting today. Cut me a break here. I already backed off, compromising with the open phone line."

I squeezed his shoulder. "And I appreciate it, but until a minute ago you were still tossing a whole lot of attitude at me."

"Yeah, I'm a guy. And a cop, trained to serve and protect. Puts an uncomfortable spin on friendships."

Laughter bubbled in my chest. "Yep, I can see that. But admit it—you'd go wonky with a bunch of clingy, dependent friends."

"True." He flicked the Jeep's turn signal. "Crozier Drive is that narrow road on the right. I'm going to travel the length of it, locate Deforest's address, then turn around and backtrack to her house. I'll find a place for the car after we've done the initial pass through. Everybody knows everybody around here, so recon is a bitch."

Well, that explained why Jace sounded stressed again. "How about approaching from the beach?"

He shrugged. "Might be an option. Let's check it out first."

There was a huge diversity in the type of houses lining Crozier Drive—some looked barely habitable, and others probably cost a fortune. Ebba Deforest's house was two stories, and set back from the road only far enough to accommodate a double garage driveway. "You can't tell much about it from here," I said, craning my neck to get a glimpse of the yard. Impossible with the six-foot fence. "We can't see a bloomin' thing from here, so I really think we should try approaching from the beach."

"I'm with you on that, Midnight. I'll park on the turn-out up ahead. There's an open area across from it that leads to the beach. It's not a public access, but I can flash my badge if someone tries to stop me."

Jace pulled onto the grassy turn-out and shut off the engine. I unfastened my seatbelt, turned to face him, and shook my head. "The beach will work for you, but how the bloody hell am *I* supposed to get inside?"

He blinked. "She didn't tell you?"

"No. Just gave me the address when we agreed on a

time." I thought for a minute. "But she's a witch. I'm going to stand in the driveway, and see if she senses my presence. If she doesn't show up within a few minutes, I'll knock on the garage door."

"And if that doesn't work?" he asked.

"I'll hike my skirt up, scale the fence, and make my presence known. She's expecting me, so it would be rude not to show up on time." I tried to look innocent, then batted my eyelashes a few times for added effect.

Jace shook his head. "You ever scaled a six-foot fence, jumped over a three-foot wide hedge, and landed on the other side without breaking any bones? Wearing slippahs?"

He had a point.

"No, but I'll definitely find *some* way to get in. I don't think I should be seen talking on the phone, though, so I should probably ring you up now."

He got out of the car and reached into his pocket for his phone. "Go for it."

I punched in his number, and while I waited for the call to connect, climbed out of the Jeep and closed the door with a solid thunk. The sound helped brace me for whatever was going to happen next, at least that was my theory.

Jace and I parted company, and I casually approached Ebba's driveway, giving myself time to scan her yard and house. The foliage here was giving off the wildest, most intense vibration I'd ever seen or felt. It was the closest thing to the purity of Universal essence I'd seen, probably because it was the result of plants, mountains, and ocean being so close to each other. They had to be sharing power. I spun in a slow circle, taking in the aura of the land. Every living thing around me was saturated with the most spiritual energy imaginable. "Gobsmacking wicked." My words rested on the breeze, then disappeared.

"Yes, it is. You must be Caitlin Connor." Her voice tapped me, the real, vibrational me, and bloody hell, if the shock of her touch didn't freeze me solid for a heartbeat or two. It was so far beyond offensive I sputtered, and then flooded my aura with pure midnight energy to create a protective shield.

In the Wiccan world, to touch someone's aura without permission was a violation of personal space so severe it bordered on assault. And damn, but her intrusion had blocked my warning chill that an unfamiliar witch had entered my field.

Solidly protected, I slowly turned to face her, while I quickly scanned her aura. *Without* touching it. Radiant. Purple with gold edges. She was one super-psychic witch. "And you're Ebba Deforest. You trespassed."

"I am Ebba. I did trespass, and I apologize. However, it is also offensive for a witch to be less than truthful with one of her own kind."

Pisser. She'd caught me out.

Chapter 3

THREE OF WANDS

Investigating new adventures.
A well-planned gamble.

EBBA DEFOREST WAS TALL, LIKE HANNAH. RECOGNIT-
ion sizzled, lighting up my nervous system. Blonde hair,
silver-gray eyes, delicate features, and bloody hell if they
weren't related, I'd... Anger flashed and I ground my teeth
to keep from saying something unforgiveable to Ebba,
especially since my irritation would be more appropriately
aimed at Hannah. I squared my shoulders, and watched
for the slightest twitch in her expression. "You're sisters,
aren't you?"

"Half. Different mothers. We have a few things to
discuss, Caitlin, and it's probably best to have this
conversation in a more relaxed atmosphere." She gestured
toward an open gate that must have blended seamlessly
into the fence when it was closed. I certainly hadn't
spotted it.

"Come," Ebba said. "Let's sit on my porch and you can
tell me why you're here."

I followed her around the side of the house, and the

beauty of the verdant foliage, coupled with the welcoming fragrances from flower beds, helped to knock my anger down a titch. The rear of the house opened to a huge covered porch furnished with a crazy mish-mash of cozy-looking, curl-up-and-chill chairs.

Ebba settled into one of the oversized seats, and motioned for me to take the one next to her. Gratefully, I collapsed into the soft cushion, and tried to quiet my mind. There was no doubt Ebba's Wiccan ability was as attuned as Hannah's, so I needed to gather my scattered senses and face her as an equal. After a couple calming breaths, I met her gaze head-on. "Why didn't Hannah tell me?"

Ebba shook her head. "That's not a fair question to begin our conversation, because I have no idea why you're asking. Why don't you start at the beginning, Caitlin, and we'll work our way through whatever has you so upset?"

"It's a long story. You know about Ted Thatcher's murder and Hannah's arrest, right?"

Her mouth dropped open, and it took a few moments before she was able to collect herself. She squinted at me, probably checking my aura to see if I'd lied. "No," she finally said. "Why is Hannah in jail?"

Puzzled, I frowned. "How do you know she's in jail?"

"Because if she weren't, she'd be here."

I filed that bit of information away, then laid out the basics for her. "They found Thatcher's blood on her hands, and on her athame. I've taken over running Ola's while she's in jail, and I'm here because I'm following clues to figure out who the killer actually is." I paused, unsure what I wanted to say next. "My instinct and Tarot readings have led me to believe the guilty person is a witch. You know the rest. You purchased an athame from Hannah last month, and your sales receipt became a lead I needed to check out."

Ebba's glare was laser sharp. "*I* did not murder anyone, but *you* have."

Pisser. My intuition was screaming that I needed this woman's help, and the only way to gain her trust would be to give her an honest and complete explanation of the incident with Fion Connor.

And Jace was listening to every bloody word. Bloomin' hell, this was *not* the way I wanted to tell him. I blew out a shaky sigh.

But maybe Ebba had enough psychic ability to see... "Yes, I was involved in a woman's death. Can you see the particulars of the...episode?" I crossed my fingers. There was a slim chance she had mind-reading ability, or like Everly, could simply touch me and witness the entire scenario first hand.

But no such luck. My insides twisted into a knot when Ebba shook her head. "I only see that you carry deep scars, and you're not malicious. I'll need to hear the details, Caitlin, but of course you know that."

In her position, I'd demand a complete confession as well. "Right. I'll list the significant points, then fill in background information if you have questions. Does that suit?"

A corner of her mouth kicked up. "It does indeed."

I stumbled through the story, my narration choppy because of the backlog of emotion that was always connected to my mother's death.

And Jace heard every awful detail. Would he even be waiting for me when my meeting with Ebba was over?

She, however, took every word in stride without a change in expression. No tight-lipped censure, no wrinkled forehead, not even a whisper of a gasp. "You carry a lot of power, Caitlin. I remember how difficult it was for me when I was in my twenties."

What? She wasn't scrambling for a phone to call the coppers. "You're not afraid of me?" Bloody hell, I sounded shaky. Not at all the impression I wanted to make.

Ebba drew her legs up, tucking them under her. "No. We're not enemies, and there's no need for us to test our power against each other. It would be a waste of time and effort, and Hannah will need both of us at full strength to get her out of this mess. Let's start with the basics; what exactly do you want from me?"

We'd wasted so much time on my past, I got right to the point. "I need to join the local coven so I can watch and listen, like working undercover."

"Hmm." Ebba pleated the fabric of her linen palazzo pants, then smoothed the wrinkles. "From what you've shared, I'm assuming the only witch you've worked with is your cousin, Everly, and that was under stressful and unusual circumstances. Is that right?"

I shook my head. "Everly isn't a witch. She could be, I suppose, but she's not like that. A Wiccan lifestyle wouldn't suit her at all."

"Covens have personalities, and are most often oath-bound. Do you have any idea what you can do with your gifts? I ask because you're a born witch, Caitlin, and there aren't many of us. For you to join a circle, and participate in, say, a healing ritual..." She paused.

I nodded.

"And you tap into your intense power—"

I dug my fingers into the soft upholstery, and held on tight. "I wouldn't do that! Not ever!"

Ebba leaned toward me, resting her hand on top of mine. "Yes, you will. The energy in a circle is beautiful, full of love and life, and it creates its own power."

Maybe she was nutters.

A corner of her mouth kicked up again. "I can see you don't believe me."

"Since the incident, I'm very careful with my midnight energy." A huge understatement.

She stood, holding out her hands. "Come, let me show you."

I heaved a silent sigh, but stood and took her hands. Better to prove my point so we could get on with the important things. "I'm ready." It was a toss-away statement, because I had no idea what she was going to attempt. Not that it mattered, since these days I never set my inside-out energy free under any circumstances.

"Close your eyes and just be. Nothing more. Nothing less."

I followed her instructions, and then scanned her energy looking for direction, very gently, and not intrusive at all. She began to glow with a warm, soft essence, an ember of pure white light. I could see no harm in letting it seep around me, as there was no malice, nothing at all worrisome about it. Within a few seconds I recognized it as the healing energy she'd mentioned earlier. And then the tension in my neck and shoulders began to drift away like shadows chased by sunlight. My body slowly became weightless, so very light, I barely felt the earth beneath my feet.

Consumed with the intoxicating sensation, I didn't notice I'd lost control of *me* until it was too late. Midnight energy had blended with the white glow, and they swirled together, creating an entirely new essence. I immediately began to draw away, to stop my dense aura from leaking into Ebba's field.

But it wouldn't stop.

A rush of adrenaline panicked me. I tried to yank my hands free. Couldn't move them.

The deepest, most dense, core of my midnight aura exploded, surrounding us, holding us, nourishing us.

Slowly my panic drained, but I still couldn't control the flow of energy, couldn't stop it from leaking into Ebba's aura.

Through the vacuum in my mind, I heard her speak. "This is what happens in a circle, Caitlin. The combined energy of several witches joins to become a new entity, one you don't have the power to control because it doesn't belong to you. The group creates, and the group dissipates. Now breathe deeply, and reach into Mother Earth."

I didn't have a better plan, so I breathed and reached. And so did Ebba. Together we released our energies and settled back into ourselves. I let go of her hands, stretched my fingers, then grabbed hold of my new pentagram. No wonder I'd been drawn to its grounding energy. "That was... I'm not sure how to describe it. Wonderful and awful, all at the same time." And it had left me befuddled, but no reason to share that bit of information.

Ebba sat down, and gestured for me to do the same. "You'll need food soon. Energy work requires physical nourishment."

I nodded, already craving a huge bowl of pasta. "So what you showed me—"

"Was to prepare you for socializing with other witches." Her smile had an enigmatic twist.

"You can get me in, then?" My voice was considerably less enthusiastic than it should have been.

"Yes, I can. I'm the Priestess of the local coven, Caitlin."

My heart splintered. Hannah had lied to me, and wasn't that absobloodylootely perfect?

Chapter 4

FIVE OF WANDS

Exhilarating combat.

EBBA TOUCHED MY FACE, HER FINGERTIPS COOL AND reassuring. "What's wrong? Surely learning I'm the priestess of the local coven wasn't that much of a shock. You've turned the color of watered-down coconut milk." She closed her eyes, probably to get a better read on my aura.

I struggled through the hurt tearing a hole in my chest to find an honest answer. "It was a shock, but not for the reason you think. You're a natural leader. True, it's only my first impression, but you guided me through that...experience, and my panic, with only a bit of a misstep."

"Your aura is frayed, Caitlin. Whatever it is has hurt you terribly."

I needed to talk about it, and Ebba was probably the only person who could help me make sense of Hannah's lie. "She told me she didn't know any of the coven members well. You're her *sister*! And the Priestess. Why would she deny knowing you?" My voice cracked.

Ebba shook her head. "Hannah didn't lie to you, Caitlin. She's never joined our coven, and *doesn't* know any of the members."

Anger sizzled. "She knows *you.*"

"Yes, but not that I'm the Priestess of a coven. It's a closed group, and all member names are strictly confidential, and besides, this is a very new coven. Most of the witches are just beginning on their journey into the Craft, and not a group Hannah would be comfortable with. She and I aren't close, didn't grow up together, and surely you've noticed I'm considerably older. If she hadn't been arrested, she might have come to talk with me, but of all the witches who shop at Ola's, Hannah would never mention my name as a possible suspect. And she knows that if I ever had, or currently have, any contact with a coven, I would never reveal anyone's legal name."

I wasn't at all happy with Ebba's response. "But you've just agreed to let me join. Why me and not Hannah?"

Ebba breathed out a sad sigh. "Hannah has chosen to remain a solitary witch. It's her story to tell, and I won't break that confidence. You have agreed to become one of us, even if it's only for a short time. You're a born witch, but have little experience with your Craft, so the group is a good fit for you. I will help my sister in any way she needs, and I plan to contact Naoko today. She's Hannah's attorney, right?"

For being *distant* sisters, Ebba seemed a bit too knowledgeable. "Yes. I met with her yesterday, and was impressed. But, if you aren't close to Hannah how did you know Naoko would be her attorney?"

Ebba's attention had shifted to the shoreline. "Why don't you ask your young man to join us? He's been waiting and watching since you arrived, and there's no shade on the beach."

She'd startled me, but only for a moment. Of course she'd sensed Jace's aura, and it was a relief he hadn't left me stranded. I reached for my phone, held it to my ear. "Hey."

"On my way." He barked out the words. Yep, the man was totally pissed off, and any hope I had for our friendship to become something more tumbled into oblivion. I rubbed at the sore spot under my ribs. How had I become so attached to him so fast?

I clicked my phone off. "He didn't know the details about Fion Connor's death until I told you."

Ebba patted my hand, and the understanding behind her eyes told me there was no need to explain further.

Jace strode toward the house, the empty beach and rolling waves a perfect backdrop for his broad shoulders and long legs. I soaked in the image, until he got close enough and I spotted his scowl. It was aimed directly at me, and cut straight through my insides.

"Oh, my," Ebba whispered. "He's quite a charming combination of annoyed masculine energy and sparkling silver aura. Psychic?"

I was almost positive Jace had some type of psychic gift, but since it would be a guess, I waffled. "I'm not sure. His father was a clairvoyant. The annoyed part is more upsetting, and—"

"Give him time to adjust, Caitlin. A homicide combined with lying by omission isn't easy for anyone to accept."

"I didn't exactly kill Fion, and I definitely didn't lie. Every official report states she died from a heart attack." I sounded obstinate, and that would never do.

Ebba stood to greet Jace. "I'm Ebba Deforest. Welcome to my home."

He shook her hand. "Jace Porter, Honolulu PD." Authority tightened his words.

Ebba gave him her quirky half smile, then sat. "Please join us. As you heard, I've agreed to allow Caitlin access to my coven."

"Seems like a good fit." He sat, his jaw so tight the muscles rippled.

"Yes." Ebba nodded. "We're not gender-exclusive, so I'll extend the invitation to you as well."

A resounding "No!" pounded in my head, but I pressed my fist tight to my mouth to keep from blurting it out. Ebba must have some reason for inviting Jace, even though he was radiating unshakeable cop assertiveness. A dozen images of him flashed through my memories, and he hadn't shown this sort of attitude in any of them. I tapped my fist against my lips.

Jace leaned forward. "I'm not a witch, Ms. Deforest."

Her raised eyebrows clearly disagreed with him. "That may be, but there's a strong possibility one of my coven is a murderer. I'm surprised, as an officer of the law, you aren't leaping at the opportunity to infiltrate the group."

Jace shifted in his seat. "It's not my case, but I'll

mention the offer—"

"It's an exclusive invitation, Officer Porter."

There was enough bite in Ebba's words to shove Jace against the back of the chair. I opened my witchy senses to take a peek at the energy flowing between them, and had to clamp my lips together to keep from smiling. There was a clearly defined, energetic hand print on his chest.

He brushed at the front of his shirt. "I see. I'd like some time to consider it, say twenty-four hours."

Irritation zapped my nerves. "It's been over forty-eight hours since the murder, Jace. There is *no* time for you to consider anything." I spun to face Ebba. "When does the coven meet?"

"I plan to call a meeting for tonight with the intention of introducing you as a Seeker. Because we have a democratic coven, I'll call for a vote whether to accept you into our family."

Anxiety mixed with excitement. "Good. The sooner the better. It doesn't matter if they accept me or not, because all I need is an opportunity to... Wait. You've already scanned everyone's aura. You must know if any of them are killers."

Ebba nodded. "Yes, before they were accepted for initiation, I did a scan with both their knowledge and permission, but all initiates have sworn to live in truth and trust, so it would be egregious for any member to scan another's aura after initiation. However, if someone in the coven has committed murder, they have broken that trust."

Frustrated and irritated, I tossed my hands up. "If I

can't scan them, how will we know who's guilty?"

The corner of her mouth twitched. I was beginning to hate her peculiar smile. "Your—what did you call it?—midnight energy? You have an inner eye, Caitlin, that doesn't require a visual aura scan to find the absence of truth and justice. It's innate." She held her palm up. "And before you discount my observation, let me clarify. When our energy merged, it became obvious because you tested me."

I stiffened. She was nutters. Gone totally 'round the bend. "That's impossible. How could I do such a thing? I watched our auras touch, yes, but I have no idea how to *test* someone."

Jace remained focused on us, his attention bouncing back and forth as we talked.

Ebba smiled, this time a full-out grin. "You'll have to trust me. Now, I'm going to get us some lemonade while you two discuss how you want to participate this evening."

Bloody hell. She'd left me alone with a steaming mad Jace.

Chapter 5

SIX OF SWORDS

Help from others.
Smooth sailing across
troubled emotional waters.

JACE GLARED AT ME, HIS EYES TURNING A DARK BROWN. "Why didn't you tell me?"

Pisser. It was a legitimate question, and that made it all the more difficult to answer. "No one's ever questioned me about the details of Fion's death...well, besides the Metropolitan Police. And then today, when Ebba asked..." I sighed, frustrated. "You're a copper, Jace. When we first met, it was a one-off thing. I didn't expect to ever see you again, and then there you were, in uniform at the scene of a homicide I was involved in. The situation wasn't conducive to spilling details about the worst moment of my life."

"There have been several opportunities since then. For example, every time we've been together." His shoulders had lowered a fraction, but there was still an edge in his voice.

Fear churned in my gut. There was nothing for it but to give Jace the details, and wasn't that a cock-up? He'd probably never speak to me again. The prospect of losing him hurt more than it should after only a few days, but he was the first man who'd ever mattered to me. I pressed a fist tight against my stomach. "It would be best if you asked me questions. I've never explained the specifics to anyone, and I...don't know how."

Jace leaned back in his chair, giving me some breathing space. "Okay, we can try that. First off, what was Fion Connor doing before her, ah, heart attack?"

Slowly, I let the sorrow and anguish of that memory fill my mind. "She was killing one of the best women I know."

He blinked. "Were you and your cousin the only people there besides Connor and the victim?"

"No," I said, shaking my head. "There were several people there, but none of them had the necessary magic to stop my mother."

Jace held his palms up. "Wait, you're saying Connor used magic to harm the victim? No weapons?"

I smiled, brittle and tight. "Magic can be lethal when it's used for harm by a powerful, seasoned practitioner. It's one of the reasons I'm so careful with my midnight energy. And no type of traditional weapon would have stopped her before she killed Siofra. Fion Connor had abnormally strong power. "

I wasn't sure, but it looked like Jace shuddered. "And you faced off with her?"

"Yes, but not alone. Everly was there and had been holding Fion in check as best she could, but when my mother realized Everly was neutralizing the murderous pattern, she turned it full force on my cousin. Everly is strong and fast, but she couldn't hold Fion off indefinitely."

Jace fisted both hands. "Is that when you stepped in?"

I sucked in a shaky breath. "Yes, Everly and I joined energy, and created a mirror of sorts that reflected Fion's lethal power directly at her. It hit her full force and killed her."

Jace shook his head. "That's not murder, Caitlin, it's self-defense."

A chill spread through me. "No matter what it's called, no matter that it was the right thing to do, my mother is dead. And I'm responsible."

The screen door opened with a swish-squeak, startling me, and I whirled to face Ebba. How much had she heard?

She set a tray of sweet-smelling lemonade on a table, then stepped behind me and rested her hands on my shoulders. "Close your eyes, breathe in peace, and exhale negativity. Let it go, Caitlin. You've been holding on to this memory far too tightly."

Apparently she'd heard everything. A deep sense of serenity flowed from Ebba's hands and seeped into every cell of my body. My eyelids fluttered shut, closing me in the dark core of my being, the place where my midnight energy originated. The panic came first. I shrugged my shoulders, then grabbed Ebba's hands, trying to force her to let go. Although her hands rested gently on me, I couldn't free myself.

Her healing energy intensified, flooding me with tranquility. I fought it, but gave up when complete solace surrounded me, absorbing the panic, one earthshaking fragment at a time. The sensation of acceptance and forgiveness was so powerful I couldn't draw a full breath.

Choked, primal sobs tangled deep in my gut, and wrenched free from a forgotten place in my soul. Helpless, I curled into myself.

Strong arms lifted me from the chair, cradled me, and every time I inhaled, Jace's wind-kissed ocean scent seeped into my senses.

The pain faded, and my midnight energy became stronger, loving, gentle. It bathed my body and mind with complete peace, the first I'd ever known.

And then my mind kicked in. I was in Jace's lap, his arms tight around me, his lips pressed to the top of my head. It was perfect until I noticed his soaked shirt under my cheek. Wet and goopy. Embarrassment flooded me, and I jerked upright, wiping the mess off my nose, cheeks, and lips. "Oh, bloody hell," I mumbled. "I've ruined your shirt."

He grinned. "Yeah. Thanks, I've always hated this shirt."

Ebba handed me a box of tissues. "Rest a minute, then I'll take you inside to wash up."

I scooted off Jace's lap, blew my nose, and mopped up most of the mess. "I..." They were both looking at me with complete understanding and total acceptance. The waterworks started again. "Loo," I whispered.

Ebba held the screen door open, and led me to a small powder room off the hall. "Take your time, Cait. A few moments to adjust to the new you wouldn't be amiss right now."

"Thanks. I—"

"Hush. Words aren't necessary." She pulled the door closed, and her footsteps faded into the distance.

I turned the water on full blast, rinsed my face, then lathered my hands and scrubbed until all traces of the tears were washed away. Water clung to my eyelashes, clouding my vision, but I managed to grope for a towel and dry off.

I folded the damp terrycloth, carefully replacing it on the towel bar, and then breathed deeply, drawing in as much calm as I could. My plan was to look in the mirror, and, no matter how painful it was, stare at myself until I'd come to terms with...me. I closed my eyes, faced the mirror, and gripped the sink edge. Cold. Hard. Like my soul used to be. I desperately wanted to be able to hold my own gaze for longer than a few seconds. It had been well over nine months since I'd really looked at myself, and it was time. If Jace and Ebba could accept the real me, so could I.

Maybe.

Determined, I opened my eyes. Didn't blink. Didn't look away. A clear, dark blue stare looked back at me. There were still remnants of the horrible black shadows that had scared the hell out of me for the past nine months, but I could face them now. Maybe even accept and integrate them with a little more time.

I finger-combed the snarls out of my hair, then tried smiling at myself. Managed a lip quirk that was way too similar to Ebba's, and then I stared right into my eyes again.

"You, Caitlin Eireen Connor, are a warrior who represents truth and justice." I gave the mirror image a determined nod, then left the solitude of the loo to face the two people who had pushed me off the edge of insanity and into the core of my soul.

Chapter 6

SEVEN OF CUPS

Bemused and confused by the possibilities.
Be careful what you wish for.

I PAUSED AT THE DOOR, QUIETLY PEEKING THROUGH the screen to determine how Jace and Ebba had reacted to my meltdown. They were sipping lemonade and chatting as though they'd been friends for years. The normalcy calmed my nerves, and I pushed the door open. The swish-squeak gave away my presence, and turning as one, they smiled at me.

Ebba patted my empty chair. "Come join us."

"I..." My communication skills had never been so shambled. I tried on an answering smile, and it worked. "I'm positively gutted. It was the first time I've cried about that day, but messy as it was, I think I'll be able to heal now." I perched on the edge of the chair, and, with a soft sigh, scooted back and let the comforting softness of the overstuffed cushions enfold me.

"How long has it been since you've cried about *anything*, Cait?" Ebba asked, handing me a tumbler of lemonade.

The glass was cool, and damp from condensation. The sensation helped keep me grounded while I sifted through my memories. "Years. I honestly don't remember the last time."

Jace grinned, and gave me a thumbs-up. "You made up for lost time, Midnight."

It was exactly the right thing to say and do. Whatever embarrassment was left over from my crying jag evaporated. "I gave it my all. And I owe you a new shirt."

Ebba set her empty glass on the tray with a loud clink. "And now that we have Caitlin sorted out, it's time to discuss your gifts, Jace."

He sputtered and choked around a mouthful of lemonade. "Excuse me?"

It had to be a witchy trick to pull off the serene, sly smile Ebba gave Jace. "Although you're not going to become a member of my coven, I am going to request your presence as an observer tonight." She sighed. "An unannounced, secret observer. It's something I've never done, and will most likely never do again. As much as secrets go against my Wiccan beliefs, I cannot allow anyone who practices dark witchcraft to remain a member."

I was a bit puzzled. "Do you think whoever killed Thatcher used witchcraft? His wounds looked like they came from a common weapon, but I still have so much to learn about magic."

She shook her head. "It would be difficult for me to know without seeing the body, but the act of killing, whether it be magical or physical, is against everything I believe in. *An it harm none* is more than mere words to me, it's a way of life."

My skin turned clammy. "But I—"

"There are several differences, Cait. You did not murder Fion Connor, you protected several other people from her lethal wrath. And you followed through by going to the Metropolitan Police and telling your story."

I opened my mouth, but Ebba held up her hand. "Leaving out the specifics regarding the necessary use of magic. You did not then, and from what I can see in your energy, you never will become a practitioner of the dark arts. It simply isn't your way."

Hope and confidence poured into every cell of my being, and for the first time since I realized I had mutant DNA, I truly smiled. "Thank you. That's the best gift anyone has ever given me."

Jace finished the last of his drink, then set the glass aside. "I'd planned to be at the meeting tonight, even if it meant becoming a temporary member of the coven, but staying hidden will work much better. I can observe the behavior of everyone who attends, and with any luck, spot something that sets off my cop radar."

Ebba straightened her spine. "Not until we've had a discussion about your psychic gifts. May I have permission to scan your aura, Jace?"

His skin had turned a worrisome color.

"You've gone a sickly shade of puce green," I said, then faced Ebba. "When I met Hannah, I learned that my body warns me when an unfamiliar witch is nearby. It's a shiver, a chill that has nothing to do with cold. It's never manifested around Jace, not even the first time I met him."

He whirled to face me, his nose wrinkled. "Good to know that happens to you, and that I'm not a witch." He paused. "What exactly is puce?"

"An odd sort of purple-brown shade," Ebba said.

I shook my head. "Nope. Where I come from it's a disgusting shade of baby poop. Not that it matters what color you've turned, I want to know *why* you're suddenly looking ill."

He tipped his head back, studying the porch roof. "Because this isn't something I talk about."

My gut twisted in empathy. "I believe I said the same thing less than an hour ago. I'll be here for you, Jace, no matter what sort of psychic gift you have." I meant it. No one had cared for me like these two people. Everly, Pierce, and Siofra were close to me, of course, but they loved me from the outside in, Jace and Ebba had accepted me from the inside out.

Jace cleared his throat. "I'm not sure how to describe it. My vision is different from normal, but—"

"I'll extend the offer again," Ebba said, taking his hand. "If you allow me to scan your aura, I can describe what I see. It might be easier for you than having to search for the right words."

Jace nodded, then slipped his hand out from under Ebba's.

She closed her eyes, and withdrew from us. It was an unusual sensation to see her sitting next to me, and not be able to feel the faintest trace of her essence. A pulse jumped in my throat. Was this what it was like for others when I scanned them?

"Jace," Ebba said. Her voice sounded distant, fragile. "Will you look at Caitlin, please?"

His beautiful ever-changing eyes focused on me, and the color shifted from pale amber to emerald. I loved watching how they transformed—so slowly it was difficult to spot the alteration until it was complete—and even then I shook my head, wondering how it had happened. Or if it was only my imagination.

"Well, then." Ebba opened her eyes and smiled. "As I suspected, your gift is in your vision. Caitlin is correct, you're not a witch, but you are a seer, Jace, and not in the usual sense. When you look into someone's eyes, you process their gaze, specifically the pattern in their iris, as though it's a fingerprint. Every person who meets your gaze leaves a genetic imprint, like DNA, and you've stored the hundreds of different patterns. When you look at someone for the second, tenth, thirty-fifth time, they immediately register in your mental data bank. Does that sound like what you experience?"

He twitched. "Yes, although until you described it, I didn't realize I stored memories and insights differently from other people. I read personalities with almost perfect accuracy through eye scans. It's unnerving. Until now I didn't realize I also retain the information, but it makes sense, and has had a profound effect on my life." He glanced at me. "It's the reason I was immediately drawn to Caitlin. I had an intense need to protect her, because there was such a discrepancy between the purity of her personality and the darkness around her heart. What I saw just now..." He swallowed. Hard. "Caitlin you are the most beautiful woman I have ever seen, inside and out."

The blush started at my feet, pink and warm, and the heat spread over every inch of my skin. Thank goodness I could only see my feet. "I'm...I don't...thank you."

Ebba stood, breaking the mood. "There's only a short time left for me to arrange tonight's meeting, so I'm going inside to call my witches. Would anyone like more lemonade?"

Jace and I both held out our glasses. Ebba set them on the tray along with her own, and Jace hustled to hold the screen door for her. Normal behavior. It brought me back to the situation at hand. "Do you have to stare into a person's eyes, or can you read them with a glance?"

"I don't have to stare, but it takes more than a few seconds for me to imprint a pattern. And I have to be close enough to actually see their eyes, so my observations tonight won't provide insight about the members' personalities." He sat, shifting his weight. "Do covens meet outside? I've heard rumors about sky clad situations..." His voice trailed off.

My stomach flip-flopped. Naked. In front of Jace. Nope, not ready for that. I licked the taste of lemonade from my lips while I decided what to say. "My understanding is that sky clad meetings are usually part of ritual holidays, and even then they aren't all that common. I haven't studied much about covens since I never thought to join one, so I have no idea what to expect tonight. I think ordinary street clothes or robes are most common, and will probably be the preferred dress for tonight."

"That's correct, Caitlin." The screen door slapped closed as Ebba set the tray of refilled glasses on the table. "My coven dresses comfortably, usually in long skirts and nice blouses or shirts."

When we had our drinks in hand, she sat, facing us. "We are a teaching coven, Cait, so you would be expected to study for a year and a day before your initiation ceremony. Tonight will be a simple introductory social. The group will want you to share why you want to join with us, how you came to choose the Wiccan path, and something about your gifts."

A chill settled along my spine. "There's no bloody way I'll explain my midnight energy to a bunch of strangers. I'm sorry if that's rude, but I can't do it."

Ebba nodded. "I agree. Have you attempted any spells?"

I shook my head. "No, but I did cast a circle to clear the energy in Ola's. I could tell them about that." It would be easy to skip over the part about Thatcher's apparition showing up.

"That will do nicely. These women aren't born witches, Cait. They've practiced different forms of the art, and treat the Craft with respect, but they're not psychic. None of them have the same level of sensitivity as you, Hannah, and I were born with. I'll keep the meeting short, have everyone share something about their personal practice, and then recommend some books for you, and arrange a time to begin your private studies with me."

Study? With Ebba? "Do you personally train everyone in your coven?"

Ebba took a long swallow of lemonade. "Yes. But tonight isn't about you actually petitioning to join us. Will the agenda I suggested give you enough time to assess everyone?"

I drew a spiral in the condensation on my glass. "I don't know, won't until we're in the thick of things."

Jace shifted position, and leaned forward. "Do you meet inside or outside?"

"It can be either, but tonight will be inside. Six members have agreed to attend. I expect both of you to respect the confidentiality of the sacred space, and never reveal anyone's identity. Jace, I'm going to ask you to stay upstairs. There's a niche where you'll be comfortable sitting, and will be able to see the circle. I'll seat Caitlin next to me on the side where you would be most visible from downstairs. Those sitting in the other chairs would have to bend and twist their necks and look up to spot you. You should be able to see everyone clearly, but be alert in case someone glances in your direction. You should also get a good view of everyone arriving and leaving, and be able to hear our conversation clearly."

Jace tipped his chin in acknowledgement. "I can work with that."

"Won't they sense his presence?" I asked. Jace packed a heavy dose of presence, both male and psychic.

"No. This is a fairly new coven. The member with the most experience has only been practicing her Craft for slightly over a year. As a group, their efforts are directed toward casting spells, healing, and divination. None of them are skilled at sensing or reading energy. That's advanced work, and most of them are still working on the basics."

"There's one last thing." I stood and collected our empty glasses, placing them just so on the tray. "I'd like to see the athame you purchased at Ola's."

Chapter 7

FOUR OF SWORDS

A temporary reprieve from duty and obligation.
Needing help from others.

EBBA BLINKED, STARTLED. "BUT WHY? THE ATHAME couldn't be connected to Thatcher's murder. In fact, it's still in the original wrapping."

I hadn't told anyone that the athame Ebba purchased was identical to the murder weapon. And I wasn't quite ready to share the information yet, but I had to focus on the truth in my answer, or Ebba would sense any prevarication. "Curiosity, I guess." That much was definitely true. "I haven't used mine except for the circle casting I did to clear Ola's, and I thought it might help to see yours." Also true. I was on a roll. "And if you don't mind explaining why you chose that particular one, I'd appreciate it." I *really* wanted to hear her explanation.

Jace shot me his I-know-you're-hiding-something look. But I wasn't, not completely. I met his gaze and did a tiny head shake.

Ebba had bent to pick up the tray, so hopefully she'd missed our silent exchange. "I'll bring it right out," she said, letting the screen door snap shut behind her.

"Questioning her integrity probably wasn't your best move, Midnight."

"I wasn't. I *do* want to understand why she chose that particular athame. There's another reason, but—"

Ebba stormed onto the porch. "It's not there! What exactly is going on, Caitlin?'

I dropped into the nearest chair. "That's what I expected. It wasn't Hannah's athame we found at Ola's, it was yours, Ebba."

She wrinkled her forehead, puzzled. "I don't understand. Of course Hannah's Craft tools would be at the boutique, because she uses them there as well as at her home. She believes that working her magic in the shop helps to keep it a sacred place for the women who shop there. She treats Ola's like it's a...coven." Ebba smiled. "I hadn't realized that until just now."

"Please sit, Ebba, and I'll explain."

Jace gave me a quick nod. "I get where you're going with this, but I'm interested in how you made the connection."

I reached across the chair, and clasped Ebba's hand. "The athame you purchased at Ola's was exactly like Hannah's, a duplicate of the murder weapon. Of course it had her fingerprints on it because it was part of the boutique inventory, but the one thing that troubles me is why your prints weren't also there."

"That's easy." Ebba shrugged. "I didn't touch it. Hannah removed it from the case, wrapped it, and, like I said, I haven't used it."

Confusion bounced around in my brain. "You purchased an athame without touching it? That's...odd. How the dagger fits in your hand, the weight, the feel of Craft tools seems so important, at least to me. You don't really know if they belong to you until you touch them." I suddenly realized I'd been running at the mouth, and to a very experienced witch. "Sorry. You know more about this sort of thing than I do. Am I wrong, then?"

Ebba freed her hand, and squeezed mine. "Not at all, but in this case I didn't purchase the athame for myself or to be used for magic. It was intended to be a gift for a friend with arthritis. She's been having a difficult time opening her mail, and that particular dagger was slim, and lightweight enough to make a perfect letter opener."

Jace scrubbed his hand over his face. "Where did you keep it, Ebba?"

And the next question burst from my lips before I could stop it. "Is it possible one of your witches nicked it?"

Of course it was the logical conclusion, but apparently Ebba hadn't made the connection. Accepting that she was inadvertently a circumstantial part of a murder would be... I didn't bother to finish the thought, because the tears pooling in her eyes said it all.

"By the goddesses, one of my coven is truly a murderer. I didn't believe it, not really. I should have sensed it, seen some sign of that sort of evil. How could I have missed it?"

"In the few hours I've known you, it's obvious you think of the coven as your family. Having a killer who's related to you is a bloody nasty situation. I did my best to avoid facing the exact same thing for most of my life, and look what happened. It turned everything arse over tit."

I breathed out some of my empathic tension when the corner of Ebba's mouth kicked up. "Yes, I'm definitely feeling arse over tit. I do believe a soak in the ocean will be necessary before this evening's meeting, which means I need some time to myself." She glanced at Jace. "And before you ask, first thing tomorrow I'll visit the detective in charge of Hannah's case to explain my relationship with her, and the athame situation."

He opened his mouth. Ebba cut him off before he got out a single word. "I'm waiting because after tonight there may be additional information I can share with him. Better it comes from me than either of you, right?"

Splotches of pink colored Jace's cheeks. "Hannah's case is being handled by Detective Adam Stone, and he's a stickler for protocol. I've been helping Caitlin in my free time, but he might not agree with my choice, so I'd rather keep my involvement on the down low unless it's necessary for me to step in."

The way Jace shifted in his chair told me how uncomfortable he was about keeping anything from Stone, and made me all the more grateful for his help. He wasn't breaking any rules per se, but helping me obviously nudged the edge of his comfort zone. Not the place I wanted to push him, so I immediately gave him a way out. "Maybe it would be best if you didn't observe tonight's meeting. It will be perfectly safe for me to come alone, and neither Ebba nor I will confront anyone. This is just a fact-finding gathering to assess potential suspects."

His glare was packed full of testosterone. "Fuck that."

There really was nothing else to say.

I WAS SURPRISINGLY CALM WHEN we arrived at Ebba's for the meeting. She'd taken Jace upstairs to show him where he could best view the entryway and listen to the goings-on downstairs, and then I helped her arrange eight folding chairs in a circle. "Are you going to call quarters for the meeting?" I asked.

"No, this will be a social gathering, so I think it's better not to add any power to the mix. If we keep it simple, it will be easier for you to get a sense of the individual witches. I'll introduce you as C...what's your middle name?"

"Eireen."

"Oh, I like that. Suits you. I'll introduce you as C.E. since you won't be expected to choose a Wiccan name until your initiation." Ebba straightened one of the chairs. "We'll sit in a circle because it works. You'll be able to see everyone, and they'll be able to see you, to help them decide whether we should welcome you as a member."

I was stunned silent. "Did you use initials for the others? Is that why you don't know their legal names?"

Ebba straightened one of the chairs. "Yes, I've always tried to protect their anonymity."

The women began arriving right at six o'clock, and everyone was accounted for by five past. Ebba ran a punctual coven, and it pleased my need for order. I listened to my body, waiting for the chill that signaled another witch was nearby, but my temperature stayed even, without the slightest hint of warning.

Ebba sat me to her right, and took my hand. "Merry meet, everyone. This is C.E. She has come to me with the intention of petitioning as a Seeker. Caitlin, please tell us why you would like to join our coven."

I didn't expect it to happen so fast, and my throat shut down. I finally managed to fumble a decent list of reasons, including that I came from a family of witches (true, but not why I chose the Wiccan path, that I had a deep respect for the Craft, had cast my first circle, and that the Wiccan belief system, as I understood it, matched my personal philosophy. It wasn't the best introduction, but it was met with nods of acceptance.

Next Ebba had each woman introduce herself, and it was all I could do to keep my midnight energy locked up tight and not scan them. Whyever had I promised Ebba I'd honor the sacred circle and not trespass? *An it harm none.* I repeated the mantra over and over as a reminder that respect for others was fundamental to the Wiccan way.

I committed the women to memory while they introduced themselves, and assigned each of them a descriptive word.

Aggie was a thirty-something strawberry blonde with a smattering of freckles across her nose. She'd dressed in a soft blue skirt and matching shirt. I tagged her with the descriptive label *soothing*. Aggie took the Craft seriously, and was a healer at heart. She seemed open and welcoming, and I dropped her to the bottom of my potential suspect list.

Clover, probably the shyest of the group, had a few

more lines around her eyes and mouth than Aggie, so I guessed her to be slightly older. She'd arranged her hair in a sort of messy topknot, just the sort of style I'd attempted to do for years, but never managed to get right. Clover was wearing ankle-length linen slacks and a woven hemp, lightweight jumper. She was definitely the earth mother of the group, so I affectionately dubbed her *earth spirit*. She slid down my suspect list to rest comfortably above Aggie.

Mara had dark hair tightly secured in a clip at the base of her neck. She'd dressed in a cobalt blue sundress that showed off surprisingly well-toned upper arms and legs. Her face was more deeply lined than either Aggie or Clover's, which was why her athletic build seemed...out of place. But then my guess about her age could be off. Mara's interest in the Craft was primarily divination, and for the entire meeting she played with a bag of runes. My descriptive word for her was *diva,* because everything she said had an arrogant twist. And when I asked if the runes were similar to Tarot, she sniffed at me. Actually sniffed. I immediately shifted her to the top of my suspect list.

Fari was absolutely normal. She selected her Wiccan name because it meant rejoice, and added that since she had plain brown hair and ordinary eyes, she needed all the joyful energy she could get. She wore bright colors, and they suited her. I liked her honesty, especially when she explained that she had no idea exactly what drew her to witchcraft, it just happened. She immediately became *serendipity*, and I clumped her with Aggie and Clover as unlikely suspects.

Salma was the oldest member of the group, maybe

fiftyish. She was also the most cautious about sharing. Her hair was cut short and had more than a smattering of gray. I recognized her skirt and t-shirt—both were patterned with lovely, complementing shades of white and off white—because they were for sale at Ola's. She wore the outfit well, and appeared comfortable in her skin. Salma was the most serious witch in the group, and her main focus seemed to center onresearch about Craft history. I named her *scholar*, and didn't have a clue where she fit in as a potential suspect. Higher than the Aggie, Clover, Fari trio, for sure.

Padmini completed the circle. She was the youngest, probably close to my age, and she was interested in communicating with spirits. Her long blonde hair and pale eyes fit well with her interests, as she appeared quite ghostlike. She gave me chill bumps, and my inclination was to keep as much distance as possible between us. Her descriptive word was *ghost*. I shifted her to the top of the list, then dropped her between Mara and Salma.

None of their names were on Hannah's list, and it took me until Padmini introduced herself before I remembered their Wiccan names were different from their legal names. Pisser. How was I ever going to reconcile them? Worse, none of the women had *felt* off enough to be a murderer. Despair clung to me like sticky tape. I'd been so sure I'd spot the killer right away.

As soon as Padmini finished introducing herself, Ebba announced she'd hold a vote about my petition in three days, giving everyone time to decide if I would fit with the group or not. And just like that, the meeting was over, because it had been impromptu, and everyone had other places to be—probably they were missing their favorite program on the telly.

I stood next to Ebba at the door while the women filed out in a flurry of "Merry part and merry meet again." Each of them smiled at me as they left, some more genuine than others, and all of them offered a socially acceptable version of "pleased to meet you."

They were obviously a friendly family, chatting together while they walked to their cars. It was probably just me, but they'd seemed far more reserved during the meeting. "Were they more tense than usual tonight?" I asked Ebba.

"Somewhat. I rarely call spur-of-the-moment meetings unless someone is ill and in need of healing, and you are our first petitioner for membership. Everyone else had spoken to me privately over a period of several months. When there was enough interest, I arranged for our first meeting and we had a group vote to decide yea or nay on forming a coven."

Well, no wonder. "I didn't sense anything from them, other than Padmini gave me chill bumps, and Mara isn't fond of Tarot," I said after Ebba had closed the door after them.

She began folding the chairs. "Padmini is young, unsettled in the Craft, and Mara's runes were a gift from her sister just before she crossed the veil. Let your impressions solidify while we clean up. Sometimes these things are more subtle, and can take time to gel."

Jace jogged down the stairs. "Learn anything?" he

asked, and picked up two chairs. "You want these back in the closet, Ebba?"

"Yes, please. Thanks, Jace."

Frustrated, I tapped a chair against the wood floor—a bit more grown up than stomping my foot. "I would have preferred an in-your-face blast of energy that rocked my midnight senses into oblivion."

Jace pried the chair out of my hands, and then winked at me.

I didn't even try to stop my grin, and then continued ranting to Ebba. "And even worse, they all introduced themselves with Wiccan names, which was very confusing. You can match their pagan names to Hannah's list, right?"

"Possibly," Ebba said. "I've never made note of anyone's legal name, because we don't use them."

"What a shambles. Where do we go from here?" I asked, bending to scoop a small glass vial off the floor.

I brought it close to my face, and the scent pierced my nose. "Bloody hell, she was here!"

Chapter 8

THE HIEROPHANT

Pursue knowledge and deeper meaning.

"WHO WAS HERE? EBBA AND JACE ASKED IN UNISON.

"My first customer at Ola's, the crabby one. I'd totally forgotten about her. Ms. Nasty had long gray hair that was skinned into a tight bun, but I don't remember anything else. I wish I'd paid more attention to her, but I just didn't. And there's no way to go back and change my scattered attention."

Ebba's eyebrows arched. "What makes you think she was here?"

I fingered the purple glass, my senses reeling. "This fragrance is synthetic lavender, and the energy matches Ms. Nasty...sort of. Or maybe it's wishful thinking because I don't have any other leads, and that punter was simply rude. Did you see who dropped it?" I handed the vial to Ebba. "I don't remember anyone moving around, or getting into their handbags, do you?"

She rubbed the glass. "Mara was nervous tonight, and

kept fiddling with her rune pouch. Maybe it fell out. Where did you find the vial?"

"Just right here." I tapped my foot on the floor, then closed my eyes and pictured the circle. "I think you might be right. This is where Mara was sitting, and she already topped my list of suspects. She seemed arrogant, but I didn't sense an absence of truth in her, nor in anyone else. I honored your request, Ebba, and didn't look at a single aura. Now I wish I had."

She sighed. "In spite of my missing athame, I didn't really believe any of these women could be a murderer. Mara is reticent and doesn't share much about her personal life, but I believe she's dating a policeman." Ebba turned to Jace. "Do you know of anyone she could be seeing, Jace?"

"Not offhand, but I'll ask around. I did pick up on a couple other things. Dark, slicked-back hair, blue dress, right? That was Mara?"

Ebba and I nodded.

Jace tapped his fist against his mouth a few times, then continued talking. "Her voice showed a level of stress I usually only hear during interrogations. It was subtle, but I also noticed her left foot twitched while she was talking. Together they triggered my cop radar that something was off with her. If she were my suspect, I'd have her in for a second interview, and she'd definitely hit my person-of-interest list."

My insides simmered with hope. "This is why coppers and witches should work together. We see different things."

Ebba nodded. "I'll invite Mara to lunch tomorrow and do some indirect poking and prodding, see if she'll willingly tell me her legal name. But you're basing a lot on a common scent, Caitlin."

"I know. I guess I'm getting desperate. But—I just remembered—this same scent was clinging to Officer Yamoto Nori when we...bumped into each other at Ola's. It wasn't like he'd been doused in it, but he wants to clear Hannah, and I think he has an idea about who the killer really is. Can you chat him up, Jace? See if he knows anything?"

"Sure. But keep in mind this isn't even enough evidence to be considered circumstantial. As in, none at all."

Frustration ate at me. "I know. But it's a starting place."

"What's your next step, Caitlin?" Ebba asked.

I didn't have to give it any thought. "If it was possible, I'd visit Hannah again, but Detective Stone said it was a one-off opportunity. Next on my list is Everly's grandfather, Kahuna Aukele. One of the cards I drew when I read Hannah's Tarot was the Hermit, and he's the only person I can think of who fits. I'm just not sure how to find him." I turned to Jace. "We should head home. I want to get an early start tomorrow, and it's been a long day."

"Finding Aukele won't be a problem," Ebba said, as she walked us to toward her front gate. "Send the request that you need him into the ethers, and he'll show up."

"You're the second person who's told me that. I'm

beginning to realize every native Oahu-ite knows the Kahuna. It's a bit unnerving. I'll meditate on sending him an ethereal message tonight before I go to bed." When we reached Jace's car, I gave Ebba a hug. "Thanks for everything. Both this afternoon and tonight."

She patted my shoulder. "We witches have to stick together."

I stepped back, shaking my head. "You sound like Hannah. I think you're more sisterly than you realize."

"I'm going to petition Detective Stone to visit her tomorrow, and you're right, Hannah and I need to spend more time together."

Jace held the car door for me, then circled around, got in, and started the engine. "You've opened new territory for me, Cait," he said, backing out of the driveway.

There was hesitation in his voice, and my heart fluttered. We'd avoided talking about our afternoon session with Ebba, instead focusing on how to handle the coven social. There'd been so much soul-baring in such a short time, it had to still be as raw for him as it was for me. Still we couldn't avoid talking about it any longer.

Guess I had to start. "Thank you for what you said this afternoon. About me being beautiful, and, um, pure. It's not how I've ever thought of myself, and it means a lot."

He reached across the seat and took my hand. "You *are* beautiful, and your energy *is* pure. We've been thrown into an intense situation without any lead-time to learn about each other. I'd like to take you to dinner, Caitlin, after Hannah has been cleared."

A date. Holy crap, he was asking me on a date. "That

would be..." I swallowed around the lump in my throat. "I'd really like that. We could fill in the getting-to-know-you gaps." And by the goddesses, I was somehow going to stop getting choked up whenever someone was *nice* to me.

Jace parked in my driveway. I was out of the Jeep before he made it around to hold my door. Before I could turn away to make a dash for the safety of my porch, he'd pinned me with a cocky smile. One I could barely see in the pale moonlight.

"It's dark. Anyone could be prowling around, and seriously, you didn't think I'd leave without clearing your house, did you?"

No question he got the dark part right. And yeah, my skin was goose bumpy, but I still didn't want to act daft and helpless. "It's fine. No one is stalking me or trying to kill me." At least I didn't think they were. Besides, what if he tried to *kiss* me? I'd had lots of guy friends, but rarely dated, what with having a psychotic mother and all. Twenty-three bloody years old, and I'd only been kissed twice, and neither of those instances was worth remembering.

Jace huffed. "Someone murdered Thatcher, and we know it wasn't Hannah. You've been actively involved in finding the real killer. Puts you at risk."

A dog barked. And it wasn't more than a yard or two away. "There are no dogs here," I whispered. "Not that I'm afraid of them, but..."

"You've only lived here a few days. Are you sure your neighbors don't own a canine or two?" Jace asked.

Footsteps rapidly approached, and a hulking male

outline moved out of the shadows and came toward us.

My blood pressure shot out of control...until I recognized his voice. "This particular dog belongs to me. Evening, Caitlin, Officer Porter."

"Detective Stone." There was no apology in Jace's voice; in fact, his tone demanded an explanation.

"Thought I'd stop by and find out if either of you had anything to tell me about the Thatcher case."

I did a double-take when the moonlight hit Stone— no uniform. Jeans, t-shirt, and the most adorable dust mop of a dog I'd ever seen was cradled in his arms. I held my hand out for him to sniff. "What's your name?"

"Merlin," Stone answered. "Your cousin rescued him during one of the cases we worked together back in North Carolina, and I adopted him. This is mostly a social visit, so I thought Merlin would help keep it...friendly."

Sneaky, but the good detective had made an excellent decision. And I certainly couldn't resist the snuffling sounds when Merlin buried his nose in my palm. I gave him an ear rub, then unlocked the door and invited the men into my home. "Have a seat, guys, I'll be right out." Right after I made use of the loo and washed the scent of fake lavender out of my mouth. Even though I'd only sniffed it, the smell had left a clingy, bitter taste on my tongue.

When I walked back into the living area, Merlin jumped off Stone's lap to greet me, and my heart fluttered like tiny butterfly wings. "Maybe I should get a puppy. Do you have any siblings up for grabs?" He answered me with an excited bark, and when I leaned down to pet him, he leapt into my arms. "Whoa. For such a little guy, you pack a bit of a punch."

Detective Stone grinned. "I volunteer at the local shelter, and one of the military families just turned in a pup that looks a lot like Merlin, but she's black. They're being transferred to the Middle East, so can't bring their dog with them. They were devastated, and asked me to help find her a home. You want to take a look?"

I shot him a sideways glance. Yep. Just as I suspected, he'd manipulated me into getting all cozy and comfortable, and damn, but it had worked. I carried Merlin to the sofa, curling into the corner with a happy dog on my lap. "I'll do that. As soon as Thatcher's killer is locked up." I suspected this situation was bloody awkward for Jace, so protected him as best I could. "I'll fill Detective Stone in on the details, Jace. After all, I'm the one who dragged you to a coven meeting."

Jace gave me my favorite of all his smiles, the one with the cheek-wink dimple. But then Stone spoiled the moment with a snort. "Lay it on me, Caitlin," he said, and hiked his ankle up to rest on his knee.

It took me a solid thirty minutes, with Jace adding intermittent observations. Stone acknowledged our narration with the occasional nod, and after I wrapped it up, he whipped a photo out of his shirt pocket, and handed it to me. "You recognize her?"

The energy in the picture was slimy, and her features nudged something in the back of my memory. Still, I was missing something. "No, but." I handed the photo to Jace. "Have you seen her?"

He squinted at the image, and I wondered if he could imprint someone's eye pattern by looking at their likeness. I filed my curiosity away for later, when Stone was elsewhere, and focused on stroking Merlin's ears. My touch interrupted the dog's soft snores, and the silence was almost painful. I held still, waiting for his raspy wheezes to start again. They'd brought immediate peace to my frayed nerves, and when they stopped, I instantly made my decision—I was definitely getting a dog. And black would be the perfect color for me.

Jace sighed, and massaged his forehead. "There's something about her." He placed his fingers on either side of the photograph, then nodded. "Yeah. The hair is wrong, but the face is right." He handed the picture back to me. "Cover her hair and check it out."

It wasn't easy with Merlin on my lap, but I finally got the photo balanced on his furry tummy and blocked out the woman's blonde hair. "It looks a bit like Mara, but that could be wishful thinking." I closed my eyes and planted the image in my mind. "Wait." I popped my eyes open. "Look at her hairline," I said, pointing. "She's wearing a wig."

Chapter 9

HIGH PRIESTESS

The embodiment of mystery.
Wisdom and insight.

"A WIG? NOT THE INFO I WAS LOOKING FOR,"
Detective Stone said. "That woman is Janice Thatcher, the
victim's ex-wife. I thought she might have shopped at
Ola's."

Pricklies broke out on my skin. "She's here? Hannah
told me the ex lives on the mainland and never leaves."

Detective Stone frowned. "Looks that way on paper,
but I thought I'd check if you or Ms. Matthews recognized
her. People travel, and I'm following up on potential
leads."

He aimed the last comment at me, and guilt slapped
me in the gut. I'd been a titch on the bitchy side with
Stone. "Thanks. I know you're trying to clear Hannah. The
lack of suspects is just bloody annoying. Did Hannah
recognize the picture?"

"It just came through from the San Francisco PD this
evening, so I haven't had a chance. Checking with her is
first up for tomorrow morning."

Merlin yawned, then blinked at me. My heart went mushy. "Where's the animal shelter? I'd like to visit that puppy you mentioned. And, before I forget, did you make arrangements for Ebba to visit her sister?"

Stone shook his head, then stood, shooting a grin at Jace. "Officer Porter can get you to the animal shelter."

Jace turned a becoming shade of pink, and leapt to his feet when Detective Stone said his name. "Can do, sir. We'll go tomorrow."

I pinched my lips together to hold back a smile.

Stone strode toward me. "I got Ms. Deforest's voicemail requesting a family visit, but I'll need to verify their relationship before the warden will okay it."

I handed the photo to him, and he pocketed it, then held out his arms for Merlin. "Got to get him home for his bedtime snack."

I cuddled the little guy for another minute then handed him over. The loss of his furry warmth had me choking back a whimper. Damn it all. I'd never had a problem with animals triggering the waterworks, but then I hadn't held a puppy or kitten on my lap since...I couldn't remember when. Nice people, and nice animals. They'd obviously partnered up to curse me with instantaneous tears. I shook it off, and walked Stone and Merlin to the door. "Will you let me know what Hannah says?" I asked. "She certainly knows Ola customers better than I do."

"I will." He handed me a card. "My cell number is on the back," he said, then shot a look at Jace, softening it with a smile. "Watch your six on the personal involvement, Officer Porter."

Jace offered his hand. "Got it covered, sir."

"There was something about that photograph," I said, closing the door behind Detective Stone. "I wish I'd snapped a picture of it."

Jace brushed a strand of hair off my face. "You're an animal person."

I caught his hand, threading our fingers together. "Do you think Ebba has Mara's address? I get that she might not know legal names, but there's a chance she'll have addresses. What if she wanted to mail them something? I want to—"

"Stalk her?"

"No." I put some oomph behind it, but Jace had that *gotcha* expression.

"You gotta stop lying, Midnight. Those cobalt eyes give you away every time."

"I wasn't lying exactly. I want to follow her, not stalk her. There's a difference." Even as the words left my mouth, I realized it was a stupid thing to say. "Sort of different. My intent is to catch her without the wig, and I much prefer the term surveillance to stalking."

He tugged on my errant lock of hair. "Uh-huh. I have several witnesses to work with tomorrow, so I'm not sure when I'll see you. I'll text when I'm free. That work for you?"

"Perfect. I'm going to focus on finding Kahuna Aukele, do my best to keep Ola's solvent, and hope Ebba learns something helpful from Mara."

He looked at me for a long minute. Some of my happy-panic must have been visible, because he planted a chaste kiss on my cheek. "There's no rush, Midnight. When you're ready, we'll know."

"I..."

He pressed his thumb against my lips. "I'll wait on the porch until I hear you lock the door."

And he was gone.

I locked the door, watched the Jeep's tail lights until they disappeared around the corner, then wandered into the bedroom, stripping off clothes as I walked. Knackered didn't begin to describe my exhaustion. So much had happened in such a short time, and bloody hell, I probably still had jet lag messing with my functioning parts. Or maybe nothing was actually working, because I still couldn't figure out what kept nagging at the back of my mind.

After I washed up, I slipped into a lightweight sleep shirt, and flicked off the light.

And immediately turned it back on.

There was a folded piece of paper sitting on the nightstand.

Adrenaline shoved me bolt upright in bed, and my feet landed on the floor with a thud. The condo floor plan was open, and I'd just had two coppers and a dog in my house, so surely no one could be hiding, but I had to make sure. I checked every cupboard, peered out all the windows, and finally breathed out a sigh. No living body other than my own was inhabiting my home. Thank the goddesses the shower had glass doors, 'cause I probably would have peed myself if I'd had to check behind a curtain.

I grabbed a pen off the dresser top, and slowly approached the night table. Until I knew who left it, I didn't want to take a chance on smudging any fingerprints. I slipped the tip of the pen between the folded edges, and read the plain block letters: CAITLIN, THE ANSWERS ARE IN THE CORE OF YOUR ESSENCE. USE YOUR GIFTS. It was signed, Aukele.

Cryptic and enigmatic. I shouldn't have expected more, and my intuition told me I wouldn't be getting any additional help from him. Irritation singed my brain cells. Why did a person have to work so damn hard to get answers in the witchy world? Step-by-step instructions would have been awfully nice. How hard could that be? And my grimoire was worse. But maybe if asking it for directions had worked once... Hope flared. That was it. I'd ask the blessed book who the killer was, and if it didn't want to answer that question, I'd ask what was nagging me that I couldn't remember.

I rushed to my altar, snatched the heavy book to my chest, and calmed my mind as best I could. "Who killed Ted Thatcher?" I asked three times, because in the Craft three-fold was a big deal. Then I sucked in a breath, and let the grimoire fall open...to a blank page.

So much for three-fold magic. One more try. "What do I need to remember?"

I opened the book, and a sprig of lavender fell to the floor.

Chapter 10

The intellectual realm of thought and communication.
The breakthrough you've been waiting for.
Be ready to act immediately.

I SLEPT WITH THE SPRIG OF LAVENDER UNDER MY pillow, thinking it might be easier for my *core essence*—as Kahuna Aukele called it—to introduce me to the killer in my dream world. Maybe even run an instant replay of me explaining to Detective Stone exactly what went down, complete with a tidy, stand-up-in-court chain of evidence. Unfortunately, I slept soundly, and woke without a single memory of any dream whatsoever.

I rushed through my morning routine, because I wanted to get to the boutique early. Since I hadn't had time to close out the register or tidy the store before I left to meet with Ebba the day before, things were in a bit of a shambles.

Images of Mara, her words and mannerisms, simmered in the back of my mind while I walked to work, made a quick detour into Starbucks, and sucked down that first happy swallow of my chai latte. It wasn't until I tripped over a crack in the sidewalk that I glanced toward the far end of the mall. A gaggle of women were hanging about outside of Ola's. "What the..." I whispered, and quickly checked the time on my mobile. Half nine. I had a good thirty minutes before the store was supposed to open.

I wasn't sure if I wanted to duck back into the coffee shop and finish my drink in peace or hustle my arse to the boutique and see what was going on. Curiosity won.

Five of them. I counted as I approached, and did an overall aura assessment of the group. The women were a virtual hive of activity that was filled with excited chatter. Their group essence radiated into a lovely pink and blue energy pattern. "Good morning, ladies," I said, strolling up behind them.

They turned to look at me, all smiles and barely controlled anticipation. "Are you waiting for Ola's to open?" I asked, while I slipped the key into the lock.

"Yes, we are. Yesterday was Claire's birthday, and we stopped by after our luncheon bash, but you were closed." Thank the goddesses she sounded curious rather than angry.

"I'm so sorry for the inconvenience. Hannah is away right now, and I had a bit of an emergency to tend to yesterday afternoon. To help make up for it, I'll let you in to browse while I set up for the day." I swung the door wide open and motioned for them to enter. Apparently it was the right thing to do, because they were busy sorting through clothes racks and chattering like magpies before I closed the door and locked it.

I set my drink down, removed my Tarot deck and the sprig of lavender from my duffle, then shoved the heavy denim bag under the counter. The cards were an advertisement of course, but today I was also planning to use them. The lavender was there to remind my unconscious ramblings about Mara and exactly how she fit into Thatcher's homicide.

I took a minute to drain half my latte while I observed the birthday girls shopping. The energy surrounding them was the exact opposite of the coven, and watching this happy group triggered an interesting idea. It still rankled a bit that I'd honored Ebba's request not to scan the members, but what if I took the complimentary colors to pale pink and medium blue... I Googled a color wheel. Pale green and medium orange were directly opposite pink and blue, and I immediately imagined them floating over the women in the coven.

The resulting image knocked the starch out of my knees, and I landed on the hard wooden stool with a painful thud. Excitement exploded. The new colors had settled over Mara and Salma like they'd been born with them. Like they were the *right* colors.

I wanted to explore my theory right off, but managed to put my impatience on temporary hold. It was going to take a while to create the scene in my imagination, and then watch it play out. And I had five customers in the store. To ensure I'd have time to explore my complimentary color idea, I needed to see to them first. "Does anyone need help?" I asked, raising my voice to carry over their chatter.

A chorus of answers floated back to me.

"Beautiful things."

"Great birthday presents."

"Claire will look gorgeous in this. It matches her eyes."

"We're fine, but will let you know if we need help."

The last comment assured me I had time to play with my experiment, at least for a few minutes. I braced my elbows on the counter, layered my right hand over my left, and rested my chin on my hand-table. I wanted to appear contemplative in case one of the women glanced in my direction. I really wanted to close my eyes, but the situation wouldn't allow that.

The next best thing was to float a gray shield in front of me to use as a backdrop for my imagined image of last night's coven group. It was easier than I'd expected, but quickly darkened to the indigo-black shade of my midnight aura. It startled me, and I tried to erase it with gray. Failed. I figured the change in color would make a bloody hash of my experiment, but then Aukele's words sounded loud and clear in my mind. This was my essence, and might be what he meant about using my gifts. I stopped fighting for control, and after the coven circle came into focus against my midnight background, I floated pale green and medium orange energy over them.

And immediately lost control of that as well. The colors morphed into a pattern completely different from what I'd expected, and I started to back out of the meditation. "Use your gift." Aukele's voice pounded the words into my mind with a virtual sledge hammer.

All right, then. I shrugged off my doubts, and focused on Mara. The green drifted away from her, making room for swirling patterns of orange. They didn't vibrate in any way I'd seen before, and wouldn't settle on a definite pattern.

Swirling orange. Memory failed me. I had no idea what it meant.

Frustrated, I shifted my attention to Salma. She was encased in a storm of dark, cloudy green. A cloudy aura was bad, and watching it made my stomach hurt...and warning tingles skittered along my spine.

"Miss? Miss?"

The strange voice penetrated my fog, and I blinked. Holy crap, one of the birthday girls stood right in front of me. *Way to go, Cait.* "I'm ever so sorry. Must have been daydreaming. I'm Caitlin. Miss is impersonal, and I know Hannah likes to welcome her customers as friends."

She smiled at me, but it was a bit forced. "We're ready to purchase these items now, Caitlin."

I gathered the clothes, exclaiming over what beautiful choices they'd made. My enthusiasm brought genuine smiles to all five faces, and then one of them noticed my Tarot deck. "Oh, look, Claire. You said you wanted a reading to celebrate your fortieth, right?"

Holy crap. I wasn't in the right space to do a reading, not with my midnight energy still on the loose. "I schedule Tarot sessions in the evening hours, right after I close the boutique to regular customers."

The birthday girl, a red-haired woman with oversized glasses, bounced to her toes. "That would be wonderful, and so perfect for my special day."

For her, maybe. "Would five this evening suit?"

"Yes," Claire said.

Her friends nodded agreement. I shuddered. "I'm sorry, ladies, but I'll need to see Claire alone for the reading."

Four smiles drooped, but Claire stepped right in to fix the situation. "We can meet for birthday drinks at OTB right after, okay? And I'll tell you all about it."

Grins all around. My head spun trying to keep up with these women's whimsical emotions. However could they keep track of their feelings?

It was a relief to hand Claire four shopping bags, each tied with a big pink bow. "Enjoy your presents, Claire. I look forward to seeing you this evening."

With a sigh, I picked up the sprig of lavender. I'd have to wait until later to research the meanings of auras that started as pale green, shifted to dark, and then cloudy, and on auras with unusual swirling orange patterns. Jace usually had his iPad with him, and would probably let me borrow it for a bit. I could use my mobile to search, but would most likely need more than one site open at a time, which was difficult to manipulate on the small screen. Plus Ola's would be getting busy, making it impossible for me to concentrate on the information.

I pushed the coven situation to the back of my mind to simmer a bit while I focused on straightening the store, and preparing yesterday's bank deposit. I'd just finished my catch-up work when Jace popped in the door with an arrangement of exotic flowers in his hand.

"Hey, Midnight. Thought you might need something special today."

"Those are gorgeous." I brought the bouquet to my

nose and inhaled. "Which one smells so good?"

"It's the ginger. How are you doing after yesterday's meeting? Have you heard from Ebba?"

Hannah kept some vases under the sink in the loo, so I headed that way, motioning Jace to follow. "I'm fine, had an interesting morning, and no, I haven't heard from Ebba yet." I filled a cut crystal vase with water, and arranged the flowers. "Hey, you had witnesses to meet with this morning, right? What happened?"

Jace took the heavy vase out of my hands. "Postponed until tonight, and my next appointment isn't for another hour. Plenty of time for you to tell me what's going on."

We strolled toward the front of the store while I filled him in on Aukele's note and my visualization experiment. I interrupted my account only to point to a round, glass-topped display rack in the center of the store. "The flowers will be visible everywhere if you put them there."

He nodded, centering the vase. "And what happened when your midnight energy showed up?"

I finished my explanation at the precise moment Jace's mouth dropped open.

He snapped it shut, then jogged to the front of Ola's, stuttering over a mouthful of words I couldn't understand. When he leaned forward to peer out the front window. I was right behind him. "What did you say?"

He didn't answer. I gave his shirtsleeve a hard tug. "What?"

"The captain just walked into On the Beach."

Jace had jogged across the boutique to watch his captain entering a restaurant? I shook my head. "He isn't supposed to eat?"

He turned away from the window and faced me. "Mara was with him. And he had his arm around her, like a lover."

Chapter 11

SEVEN OF SWORDS

Defend your position and guard your assets.

I WAS MISSING SOMETHING. "EBBA TOLD US YESTERDAY that Mara was dating a copper. Is the captain married?"

"No," Jace said, moving away from Ola's front window. "Widower. His wife passed on a couple years ago, of cancer. It left him damn bitter, and he's been a bear to work for ever since."

"So..."

A tiny smile touched his lips. "Tapping into that midnight energy of yours must have wiped out some stored data."

Heat pooled in my cheeks. What in the bloody hell had I missed? I sifted through my memories, starting with the most recent and worked my way back. It took a solid five minutes before I bumped into the conversation Jace and I had just before I set up our first meeting with Ebba, when he'd told me Stone had been taken off the case. "Holy crap. Your captain was protecting his girlfriend. That's why he took Detective Stone off Hannah's case. Do you think he knows Mara is a murderer? Would he send an innocent woman to jail on purpose?" My voice rose with every word. "I want to meet this captain of yours, maybe mess with his energy, and—"

Jace slapped his hand over my mouth. "Don't even think it. You're not that kind of witch, Caitlin."

I shoved his hand away. "I stand for truth and justice, so I damn well *am* that kind of witch." Power swelled in the core of my being, and my midnight energy shimmered with it, plunging me into my birthright.

And then the wind started.

It wrapped me in a spiraling vortex that knocked Jace into a display rack. T-shirts flew off a nearby table, and with the next gust, my hair whipped around my face, blinding me. Frantic to stop it, I sucked in a breath and reached for the earth the way Ebba had taught me. The wind calmed, but not enough. I grabbed my ceramic pentagram, held the pendant tight in my hand, and tried again, this time breathing deep into Mother Earth.

A customer peeked in the window.

By all that's holy, don't come in here! I screamed the words silently in my head, and desperately reached deeper into the earth. The tornado subsided to a gentle breeze. I inhaled, shaky, and thrust my hair away from my face. My insides churned and tumbled like they'd forgotten where they belonged.

The shop door opened. Bad, bad timing. "What time do you open tomorrow?" A high, tinkling voice asked.

Jace must have answered, because the woman smiled before she backed out of the shop.

I breathed a sigh of relief and tried to get my emotions to stop spinning. Conflicting reactions seethed in my mind: surprise, respect for the power, humility, and under it all a solid base of panic. What if I'd hurt Jace? Or that innocent customer?

Jace watched me from a few feet away, arms crossed, head cocked to the side. "Hell, woman, you pack a wallop."

That was it? "You aren't hurt or...terrified?" I sounded like a feeble old woman. That wouldn't do at all.

"Hurt? No. Terrified? Damn straight. But I'd have to be fucking stupid to let it show before you controlled the power."

I moved toward him, cautiously at first. He didn't back away, so I threw my arms around him, and hugged him tight. "Thank the goddesses I didn't hurt you." I leaned back to see his face, his eyes. They were the color of the ocean on a stormy day.

He tucked my head under his chin. "Is that gonna happen every time you want to fix injustice?"

It was a logical question. "I have no clue. What I *do* know is the first thing I'm going to beg Ebba to teach me will be control." I stepped out of his arms, and the loss of his strength and warmth left an empty spot in my chest. "It helps that you didn't panic and run away."

"Couldn't. Somebody had to bar the door, keep you from storming into OTB and handing out the Caitlin brand of justice. Someone might misunderstand." He grinned, complete with a cheek-wink.

And I knew it was going to be all right. As long as neither the captain nor Mara crossed my path. "So their relationship..." I pointed toward On the Beach. "That's proof Mara killed Thatcher. Why else would the captain take Detective Stone off the case? He was protecting his girlfriend. Now all I need to do is—"

"We."

We were still a team. Still friends. Strength and courage flooded me. "*We* need to find enough evidence for Stone to arrest her. Which means I should fill Ebba in before she visits Hannah. Surely one of them will know Mara's legal name, and I...*we* will be able to track her down, and figure out why she murdered him."

Jace pulled his phone out of his pocket and checked the screen. "I need to get to my next appointment. You can't call, but sweet Jesus, after this..." He tossed his hands up. "Text when you hear from Ebba. I don't want to spend the rest of the day worrying you're off creating tornados, especially around the captain." He narrowed his eyes. "Promise you won't look out the window. If you spot him with Mara..."

"There's no telling what I'll do," I whispered. Yes, I wanted justice for Hannah, but at this stage of making friends with my power, I'd just mess up her case. And that possibility scared me to bloody hell and back. "I'll text you when I hear something. I promise."

"And you'll stay away from the window?"

"Yes." There was something... "Oh. I almost forgot. Can I borrow your iPad, please? I want to do some research on aura colors, and it's difficult to swap between sites on the phone."

"Sure. I'll be using a sketchpad and the computer at

the station for the rest of the day. Be right back." He'd nabbed a parking place a few doors down from Ola's, so was handing me the iPad in less than a minute. "It's fully charged, so I didn't bring in the power cord, that okay?"

I nodded. "I'll only be able to run searches between customers, so I'm sure it'll be fine."

Jace pulled me to him, and kissed my forehead. "Later, Midnight."

Two seconds later the shop was flooded with punters...ah, customers. I was that close to remembering several American-speak words. In any case, they kept me busy until half-one. By the time Ola's finally emptied, I was desperately hungry. Apparently unleashing a storm of midnight energy had increased my metabolism to the starvation point. I'd overheard some Starbucks customers talking about the rich, creamy taste of the locally caught fish, and I wanted to sample it, so, as Jace had suggested, I rang up OTB to place an order for opah salad. They were happy to accommodate me, and promised delivery in twenty minutes.

I used the precious minutes for research on the meaning of aura colors. Usually I assigned my own interpretations because the energy spoke to me in its own way. But this was an experiment, and I didn't trust my intuition. After reading through several descriptions, I made some notes on the pad I kept next to the cash register.

Dark green and cloudy—jealous, resentful, unwilling to accept responsibility for actions.

Pale to medium orange—impatient, acting without

considering the consequences.

There hadn't been time for me to make any notes on my earlier vision, but I remembered the orange had settled around Mara, and I quite happily checked off another mark next to her name in my probable killer column. She'd most certainly acted with a lack of concern as to the consequences of murdering her ex-husband. That made three marks against her: the wig, her uncanny resemblance to Janice Thatcher, and, if my deductions were correct, she was impulsive to a fault.

There was only one problem: not a single item on my list was admissible-in-court evidence.

An OTB waiter strolled into the shop and, with a flourish, set my salad on the counter in front of me. "Good choice for lunch. The opah was fresh-caught this morning." He checked the sales slip. "That'll be fifteen-sixty."

I dug the money out of my wallet and added a generous tip. "Thanks. I appreciate you running it over here."

He held up the cash. "Any time."

I unwrapped the plastic fork and took my first bite of native fish and crisp lettuce. The opah was rich and buttery, a bit like tuna or swordfish, but with a melt-in-your-mouth texture. After a couple more bites that I washed down with half a bottle of banana coconut juice, I went back to work. Well, tried to go back to work, but had to set my notes aside when two women came into the shop. Twins. Their features were mirror images, except for the hair. One had long, blonde, wispy strands, and the other short-cropped, light brown layers.

"Welcome to Ola's," I said, contemplating how much difference hair style and texture made. "Are you twins?" The question slipped out before I realized I'd been comparing the women to Mara and Janice. "I'm sorry. I didn't mean to pry, but you look so much alike." No point mentioning my curiosity had spun out of control.

The blond nodded. "We are twins, fraternal obviously. I have my mother's hair, and Suzi has dad's. We had to wear hats to fool our parents when we switched identities."

"And our dates," Suzi added.

They focused on shopping and left me to contemplate the Janice-Mara issue while I made quick work of finishing my salad. The twins were in dressing rooms, so I stepped outside to toss the empty cardboard container in the public trash bin. It wouldn't do to have Ola's smell like fish, no matter how good it tasted.

The twins were ready to check out a few minutes later, and left the store with two bulging bags which had added a nice boost to the daily take. While I tidied up after them, I considered what sort of Tarot spread would best clarify the Janice-Mara issue, and decided on one I'd read about but never used. It had a strange name, but I couldn't remember the particulars, so flipped through the pages of my favorite Tarot guide. Good thing I'd tossed it in my duffle before I left the house. Sometimes luck was on my side. Now if it would just carry that positive energy into a reading.

I ran my finger down the list of layouts, stopping at

the Hanged Man's Hugin and Munin spread. No wonder I hadn't remembered the name. According to the book, they were the names of Odin's raven messengers, and meant *thought* and *memory*. The spread was designed to compare a current situation with a memory, and to clarify any connection between the two. It would be perfect for checking on Mara's presence in the coven, what happened in the past to require her use of a wig, and maybe it would even show me a connection between the two.

I shuffled the cards, cut them, and pulled two. The King of Wands reversed represented Mara's current situation, and the Nine of Wands her memory. The King stood for force and aggression, and would do anything to make a point. The Nine told of planning, defending a position, and guarding assets. So Mara was in a place where she'd do anything to make her point, and that decision came from needing to protect herself. I'd over-simplified it, but sometimes simple worked best.

Thinking back to what Hannah had shared about Thatcher's love life, it fit Janice perfectly. As the ex-wife of a violent man, she'd probably needed to protect herself, then over the years she'd healed, gotten stronger, and was ready to face him and demand revenge. But would she have murdered him to make her point? It was a huge leap.

Sliding the two cards back into the deck, I absentmindedly shuffled. It helped me think when my hands were busy, and the energy of my Tarot cards was calming. My theory about Mara would only work if she and Janice were the same person. I set my deck down and grabbed my mobile. It was way past lunch, and Ebba hadn't phoned or texted me. The lack of communication was beginning to give me knots in my stomach.

Surely Mara hadn't...hurt Ebba. I didn't want to ring her up and chance disturbing the two of them if they were having a late meal, but I needed to know Ebba was okay. I hurriedly typed a message: **You safe? Mara's surname?**

My mobile buzzed immediately. Message not delivered.

What did *not delivered* mean? Was Ebba's phone turned off? The knots in my stomach sent warning tingles over my skin. Something was seriously wrong. I couldn't ring Jace up because he was working with witnesses. Detective Stone? He'd promised to fill me in on Hannah's reaction to Janice Thatcher's photo. Where had I put his phone number?

I set the Tarot deck down, and bent to rummage through my duffle. Surely I'd tucked Stone's card in the side pocket before I left home. The stiff paper had worked its way tight into a corner, so it took me a minute to dig it out.

When I finally straightened, the scent of synthetic lavender hit my nose. I let out a stifled scream.

Mara stood on the other side of the counter.

Chapter 12

THE MOON (1)

Tap into the power of lunar magic.

I INHALED A PANICKED BREATH, THEN PLASTERED A shaky smile on my face. If it weren't for the nasty off-scent of the lavender I wouldn't have recognized her. Long gray hair. No wig. And yes, she'd been Ms. Crabby Customer. "You scared me, Mara."

Couldn't let her know what I suspected. Without the wig, she looked...familiar, obviously like Ms. Crabby, but also like...Salma, maybe.

I needed to act normal. Like I didn't remember her from that first day. Like we were potential friends and coven mates.

Mara frowned. "You were down there on the floor, and not paying attention."

The accusation fit. "Yes, I misplaced a business card." There was no way to deny it, since the thick, paper rectangle was clearly visible in my hand. I tucked it beneath the Tarot deck. "Are you here to shop, then?"

"No. I came to see you." Venom saturated her voice.

"It would be best if you withdraw your petition to join our coven. You don't belong with us, C.E. You're a misfit."

Not what I'd expected her to say. "I don't understand." I deliberately left my response open so she'd have to explain, and maybe give me a clue as to Thatcher's killer.

Mara pointed at me, her finger shaking. "That says it all. You're not one of us, so of course you don't understand."

"But I am Wiccan. And I want to study with Ebba. Why don't you think I fit with the coven?" Out. I needed to get her out of Ola's, but I couldn't push or she'd get suspicious. Chills crawled down my back. Where the hell were all the bloody customers when I needed them?

She sniffed. "Maybe. I just don't like you, and I'm going to vote against having you join us."

My intuition finally kicked in. Mara's behavior was the exact opposite of last night. "What happened to change your mind? You seemed to like me last night."

Her lips quivered. "Just go away. You need to go away."

Mara's eyes had glazed over with an eerily familiar scary look, the one Fion had while she was trying to kill Siofra. I shoved my panic aside, and focused on finding the woman beneath the insanity. "I live here, Mara," I said, keeping my voice very gentle.

"Hannah has to die. You understand that, don't you?"

Not in this lifetime. "Why? Has she harmed you?"

Mara raised her arm, her fist clenched tightly around a vial. "Ted loved her. Wanted her. But he's mine. Will always be mine."

She threw the vial at me, missed. It shattered against the wall directly behind me, filling the shop with the horrible odor of fake lavender.

Mara grinned. "There. I fixed it. This store has always smelled like delicate, spicy, lavender. Now I've made it *mine*. Not Hannah's. *My* very own perfume."

I sneezed, then swallowed bile. The damn stuff was making my eyes water. "You." Another sneeze. "Made the perfume?"

She preened. "Well, yes. I had to make Ted understand I was the better woman. That I could create what Hannah could only buy, bitch that she was."

The shop door opened, and Salma sauntered in. "Mara, I didn't expect to follow you here."

Mara mashed her lips together, and gripped the edge of the counter. "Just suggesting to C.E. that she withdraw her petition to join our coven."

Salma's eyes glittered with hatred.

Bloody hell, I was in major trouble. And worse—or maybe better—my midnight magic was seething to be set free. I eyed my mobile. Could I text for help while they were facing off with each other?

"An excellent idea," Salma said.

I picked up my mobile. "You've made your point. I'll just ring Ebba up and—"

Salma snatched the phone from my hand, and dropped it in her pocket. "That won't be necessary."

Pisser. I really didn't want to murder either of these women. But my magic had leaked out when Salma touched me, and it took all my strength not to blast her with it. "It's a simple phone call, Salma. Then you and Mara can be off doing whatev—"

The shop door swung open, and in popped Claire, all smiles and sunshine. Adrenaline sent chills skittering through me. Bloody, bloody, hell. Why had I wished for customers? And what was she doing here so early? How she missed the malice surrounding Salma and Mara was a mystery, but more than that, her survival instincts must have been nonexistent. "Claire, hello. I wasn't expecting you until later." I held my voice steady and even, so as not to spook Salma.

Claire bounced to her toes a few times. "I know, Caitlin, but I had to get here early. I'm so excited, and I want to get a small gift for each of my friends before my reading. Something to remember my birthday, and meeting you, and sharing Ola's with them. It's all just so perfect." She actually squealed.

Panic clouded my common sense, and for a minute I had an overwhelming urge to gag her.

Salma glared.

Claire was oblivious. "I'll wander around and select some presents," she said, giving Salma and Mara a wiggly finger wave.

"Get rid of her," Salma hissed.

Good suggestion. "How? She's a regular customer, and she has a reading scheduled in..." I had no idea what time it was, but my stalling seemed to work.

Salma grabbed Mara's arm. "Get that woman out of here, or you'll be meeting your dear husband in the next few minutes."

That wasn't going to happen. Whether by choice, or my inability to control it, my midnight energy had coiled and...

Mara jerked free, and backed away, snarling. "No. I won't protect you any longer." She tossed the bag of runes on the floor. "And I won't carry these horrible things around. They're cursed. You said they'd keep us safe, but you hurt Ted. We weren't safe at all."

Salma pointed a dagger at her, the double-edged blade flashing in the shop's overhead lights.

I breathed in, grounded my essence into the earth, and directed a handful of my coiled energy at Mara's chest. She crumpled to the floor a heartbeat before Salma plunged the dagger into the empty spot where she'd been standing.

Stunned silence sucked everything into slow motion for a nanosecond. And then my phone buzzed. Salma blinked at me. And Claire twittered from behind a clothes rack. "Is everything all right over there? Did you drop something?"

I sucked calm from the earth through the soles of my feet. "Everything's fine," I called to her, hoping she would stay behind the clothing display.

Salma yanked my phone out of her pocket, and glared at it. "Well, well, well. I got here just in time. That bitch, Ebba, has sent you an interesting message, *Caitlin*." She spit my name out. "There's power in a name, and now I know who you *really* are." Salma glared at me, evil spilling from behind her eyes. "The timing is excellent, and fits right into my plan."

Claire peered over the top of the clothes rack. "Do you need any help?" she asked, before disappearing back behind the display.

"No, but thanks." Damn I hadn't meant to shout. I swallowed. "It was one of Hannah's heavy Hawaiian history books. It's all tucked away where it belongs."

Salma's mouth twisted in an evil smile. "You're good. Too bad you lack dark magic."

I didn't have time to catch my breath before she mumbled something, words that uncloaked her aura.

The force of an angry black tempest knocked me back a step, panic surged, and then the familiar, telling chill spread through my bones, the one that signaled another witch was near. Complete calm seeped into my mind, and two thoughts whirled to the surface: Salma was a bloody vengeful witch, and demonic energy was nothing like the essence of my midnight core. I summoned my power, fully prepared to fight this witch with every ounce of magic at my command.

Her eyes glittered with excitement. "It will be such a pleasure to kill you." Salma tossed my phone on the counter, then shoved the dagger into her pocket. "One witch to another. I've prepared all my life for a chance like this. All the blood I've drained from witches. Every ounce I've spilled and consumed with malice. This is the moment when I can finally test the power, the elixir so many lives has provided. "

She unleashed a blast of seething black fire.

I froze it with a smile. Stolen magic wasn't true, and it would never belong to Salma. I dipped into my midnight essence, opened my body to receive it, and held up my hand, sending the blast back to her.

She shrieked.

Detective Stone burst through the front door of Ola's, backup flanking him, all weapons drawn. "On the floor. Hands behind your head. Do it now," Stone shouted.

Salma growled at him, gathered a new sphere of malignant energy, and raised her arm to throw.

Stone shot her. In the chest. Dead center.

She struggled, her face a mask of surprise, and then stumbled and landed in a heap next to Mara.

Mara groaned.

"Thank the Universe I didn't kill her," I mumbled.

Detective Stone stared at me. "What? Are you injured?"

Claire ran out from behind the clothes rack, took one look at the two bodies on the floor, and promptly fainted.

It was going to be a long evening.

Epilogue

THE MOON (2)

*The waning moon is the time
to complete unfinished work.*

AN HOUR LATER THE SHOP WAS NEARLY EMPTY.
Paramedics had taken Salma and Mara away, and law
enforcement had cleared the area, except for Claire and
me. After she came to, I took her to one of the dressing
rooms and talked her down from her fright, then gave her
a mini birthday reading. Detective Stone spent a few
minutes with her, probably taking some kind of statement,
and with a sigh of relief, I shooed her on her way with four
complimentary (Ola's could afford the loss) gifts for her
friends, and the promise of a free reading the following
week.

Good thing I'd flipped the Open sign to Closed right
after Claire fainted, because a few people were rubber-
necking when I locked the door behind Claire. I watched
to be sure she made it to her car without incident, and
then gratefully curled into one of Ola's comfortable chairs
to face Detective Stone's questions. He perched on the
stool behind the checkout counter, iPad in hand. "Start

from the beginning."

His voice rose at the end of the statement, turning it into a question. I went for it. "You first. Who were Mara and Salma in real life?"

He shook his head. "Can't release that."

Frantic pounding interrupted him. It was Ebba, twisting the doorknob this way and that, her face pressed close to the glass. I jumped up to let her in. Maybe Detective Stone couldn't talk, but Ebba certainly would. "Hey," I said, wrapping her in a hug. "I was so worried when you didn't phone or text."

"I was with Hannah, and those guards confiscated my cell before they'd let me see her." Ebba's voice trailed off when she spotted Detective Stone. "What happened? I'm too late, aren't I?"

I made quick work of filling in the details of what went down, then summarized where we stood. "Mara is probably going to be okay. Salma is in critical condition. Both of them are under guard. Mara's runes were apparently a cursed gift from Salma. I'm guessing the dead sister was a cover story to keep you from looking too closely at them?"

Ebba nodded. "Yes, that makes sense now. Mara lied about them, probably to protect Salma."

I glanced at Stone. He was getting twitchy, so I hurried things up. "Detective Stone, here, is about to take my statement, but I'm going to need something to drink first. I'm about knackered out. Anyone else want—"

Jace rapped on the door, a cardboard container holding Starbucks cups balanced in his hand. I rushed to let him in. "My savior," I said, grinning.

He looked me over, crown to toes and back. "Are you hurt? I heard right after I finished interviewing my last witness, and—"

"Broke the speed limit getting here." There was an edge to Stone's voice.

"Yes, sir, I did. You would have done the same," Jace said, handing his boss a cup of coffee. "Just the way you like it, black, extra hot."

Stone shook his head, and took the cup. "You might as well have a seat." His phone rang, and he set the coffee down, then walked outside to take the call.

Jace handed out the drinks, minus one for Ebba. "Sorry, I didn't know you were here, Ebba."

"I have it covered, but thanks." She pulled a bottle of water out of her handbag, and Jace headed for the dressing rooms to get a stool. Ebba had already settled in the oversized chair next to the one I'd reclaimed.

I turned to her. "What happened with Hannah? Did she recognize the photograph of Janice Thatcher?"

"Yes." Ebba grinned. "Mara *is* Janice Thatcher, which makes her Ted Thatcher's ex-wife."

Detective Stone barreled back into Ola's and cleared his throat.

I ignored him. "But she didn't kill her husband, Salma did. So who the bloody hell is Salma?"

Stone cleared his throat again.

"What?" I snapped at him. "You won't tell anything, and I need to get the facts straight before I give you my statement."

"Damn if you're not an Everly clone. Salma is Jo Hyde. She's Janice Hyde Thatcher's sister, and Ted's sister-in-law. Interesting phone call I just got. Janice Thatcher hasn't stopped talking since she got in the patrol car."

He was deliberately poking at my curiosity. And it was working. Worse, he knew it. "Your eyes are twinkling, Detective. I think you're enjoying this way too much."

It was the first time I'd seen Detective Stone grin. Real. Genuine. He was growing on me, and he loved Merlin, which scored him big points. So I winked at him. "I see why Annie loves you."

And that made him blush the sweetest shade of pink. Score one for me.

"Okay," he said. "Here's the deal. Janice was obsessive about Thatcher. She controlled the insanity for a few years after their divorce, then tracked him here and started following him. When she realized he was interested in Hannah, she started shopping here. Enter her sister. Jo Hyde thought she'd fix everything by killing the man who had driven Janice insane, and by framing Hannah, would give Janice the revenge she needed to heal. Jo hated Thatcher, because Janice fell apart when he divorced her. Jo had essentially lost her only sister."

I drew in a long breath. "Which means Jo is just as nutters as Janice. Must be genetic."

He gulped half his coffee. "Just got the info. A canvass of Janice's neighbors turned up most of the facts by early this afternoon. Fortunately I called in a favor last night, and one of my friends had been running surveillance on Janice, aka Mara. Wouldn't have made it here in time otherwise." There was an undercurrent of warning in his words.

The man had probably kept me from unleashing my midnight energy to do harm. And I owed him. "I'm sorry I snapped at you," I said to Stone. "It's been a rough day, and I...I'm sorry. How about I give you my statement now?"

After Detective Stone was satisfied he had all the facts, he left, with a warning to stay out of police business. Of course I promised to do my best. And then I took Ebba's hand. "What will happen to your coven now?"

"I've chosen to disband it. Hannah and I had a long talk, and have agreed to begin working together, both with our magic and to learn about each other as sisters." Her smile was the most content I'd seen. "And now that I've seen firsthand what sisters can do to each other, well, I want to make sure Hannah and I communicate, and become friends. It's a bond too special to waste."

"Oh. That's really good news." I tried to keep the disappointment out of my voice.

"Considering you just heard good news, you're looking a little droopy, Cait."

"It's just that I wanted to study with you. I have so much to discover about the Craft, and I really need to learn how to control my magic after...you know. I told you about the scene with Jace."

He leaned toward Ebba. "I would appreciate it if you'd take her on as a student. The woman can be fucking wild." He grinned, so I knew he wasn't all *that* scared of me.

"Hannah and I would love to have you join us. A mini

coven of sorts, and three is a special number for witches." She stood. "I need to get back to the jail, so I'll be ready to bring Hannah home with me when they release her. These first few days away from prison, I don't want her to be alone."

"May I visit?" I asked.

"We," Jace added.

"Of course. Why don't you join us for dinner in a few days? We can make it a celebration." Ebba bent to give me a hug.

"Do you allow dogs in your home?" I asked, slipping a glance at Jace. "I'm hoping Jace will take me to the shelter tomorrow. It's Sunday so the shop will be closed, and—"

"I'll pick you up at nine tomorrow morning," he said. "I'm off, so we can spend the day organizing you and your new family member."

I was seriously falling for this man. He had all the right moves, and words. "Thanks."

"And the new addition to your family will be welcome in my home," Ebba said, turning to wrap her arms around Jace. "You're welcome to visit any time, Jace. And I thank you for taking care of Caitlin. She's come to mean a great deal to me, and to Hannah." She hurried out the door, giving us a quick wave before she pulled it closed behind her.

Jace took my hands. "You mean a lot to me, too, Midnight."

My heart swelled, and for the first time kindness didn't jumpstart the waterworks. Deep gratitude and happiness blossomed around my heart. I stretched onto tiptoes to brush my lips against Jace's mouth, then leaned back. "Now that's real magic."

A beautiful shade of turquoise sparkled in his eyes. "An it harm none."

A Note from L.j.

Dear Readers,

There will be three episodes in each of Caitlin's Wiccan adventures, and I look forward to sharing them with you.

Happy reading...and, as always, you have my thanks for reading Caitlin's first adventure. I hope you enjoyed it. You can reach me...

Website: www.ljcharles.com/

On my website there's a form to subscribe to my newsletter. I send them out to announce new releases, cover reveals, Facebook events, book signings...that sort of thing. So if you're interested, please sign up.

On Facebook: www.facebook.com/ljwrites

On Twitter: @luciejcharles

Proof

62096736R00154

Made in the USA
Charleston, SC
01 October 2016